"I've Never Kissed A Fireman Before."

Gabe whispered the words softly.

Caroline giggled, a happy, infectious sound bubbling from in her throat. Gabe stopped cold, then a slow answering smile touched his lips as he moved away. Gazes met, clung, challenged.

"Laugh, lovely lady. I can wait." He brushed sooty ash from her cheek. He'd never felt like this, and he'd rushed her, but he wouldn't again. "I can wait, but I promise you, for us there will be kisses with laughter."

Caroline's smile faltered; her brow puckered in a frown. "I'm afraid you've made a mistake; my gratitude doesn't extend to what you seem to want."

"No mistake," he murmured. "And it's not gratitude I'm looking for."

Dear Reader,

Season's Greetings!

This holiday season is one we associate not only with the hope for peace on earth and goodwill to all, but with love and giving. Perhaps the greatest gift is the gift of love—and that's what romance is all about.

The six Silhouette Desires this month are a special present from each author, and are for you, with love from Silhouette. In every romance, the characters must not only discover their own capacity for love, but the ability to give it fully to another human being. Sometimes that involves taking great risks— but the rewards more than compensate!

I hope you enjoy Silhouette Desire's December lineup, and that you will join us this month and every month. Capture the magic of romance—the gift of love.

Best wishes from all of us at Silhouette Books.

BJ JAMES
Twice in a Lifetime

Silhouette Desire

Published by Silhouette Books New York

America's Publisher of Contemporary Romance

SILHOUETTE BOOKS
300 East 42nd St., New York, N.Y. 10017

ISBN: 0-373-05396-7

First Silhouette Books printing December 1987

America's Publisher of Contemporary Romance

Printed in the U.S.A.

Books by BJ James

Silhouette Desire

The Sound of Goodbye #332
Twice in a Lifetime #396

BJ JAMES

married her high-school sweetheart straight out of college, and soon found that books were delightful companions during her lonely nights as a doctor's wife. Her life is filled with her loving husband and family, pets, writing...and romance.

One

Beautiful," Gabe Jackson murmured as he leaned lazily against the smooth wood of a massive porch railing. A smile touched his lips, easing the tenseness of his mouth and crinkling the darkly tanned flesh about his eyes. A fine webbing of lines scored his temples, evidence that once laughter had come easily to him.

From the shelter of the old inn's veranda he watched as sunlight burned through the shrouding mist that rose in the wake of an afternoon rain. Accustomed to the dry glare of desert sands he stood, fascinated, as sunshine poured like heated gold over the mountains and through the valley. For as far as his weary eyes could see, there was only the dappled green of rolling hills and the blue of a rainswept sky. A nearby stream rushed past in a whisper, a lonely hawk cried. They were a part of a timeless world.

Gabe was tired. He hadn't known how tired, until the day he'd first come to Stonebridge. That was months ago. He'd traveled from halfway around the world to attend the last rites for an uncle, ancient, little known, and the last of his family. Adrift and oddly, profoundly alone, he'd felt the lure of the quaint village. With an effort he'd shaken off the pall of death, reminding himself that the loss of this stranger left him no more solitary than he'd ever been. He needed no roots, no family, nor did he need tranquility. His world was exotic, exciting and turbulent. Solitude and danger were his life; he sought no refuge from them.

Yet in the passing months his world had suffered a change and he'd returned to Stonebridge, seeking the refuge once rejected. It was here that he would spend the remaining months of an enforced and confining recuperation.

Hooking the rung of a rocking chair with the tip of his shoe, he slid it toward himself. Sighing contentedly he slumped into it, propping his feet one over the other on the white banister. The battered hat he wore tilted over his forehead, and his chin drooped toward his chest. Long fingers laced and rested loosely at his waist. His mind held no thoughts but of the quiet.

From deep in the woods the drumming of a woodpecker began, answered by the sleepy grumble of a nearby gander. Sounds from the wild and the muted clatter of glassware from the dining room rose and fell about him. A pungent scent of pine mingled pleasantly with the aroma of food drifting from the kitchen. And there was laughter—soothing music that Gabe heard without listening.

A remnant of thunder rumbled, its echo rolling and twisting about the rooftop. Building, easing, building again, it roared to a battering crescendo. A chandelier swayed, tinkling wildly. Crockery rattled hollowly. Great pots of ferns shook in their stands. The floor shifted and creaked, the inn seemed to tremble on its foundation, then shuddered sickeningly and was still.

Trouble!

"Hell!" Gabe muttered, his drowsy mind clearing as he bounded to his feet. The move sent the rocker tumbling, his hat fell unnoticed to his feet. Cautiously he waited, alert, ready, wishing the furor could have been thunder. In a half crouch he searched for the source of rising sound and braced himself for a second explosive shock that did not come. Instead a shower of sparks and ash began to fall as thickly as snow.

"What the—"

"Mr. Jackson!"

Gabe spun toward the young bellboy he'd met on his arrival the night before. "Yes, Tim?"

"Shiloh—" Tim took a long breath to calm himself, then began again, repeating his instructions in a hurried, stuttering garble. "I mean Mr. Butler asked me to tell—to warn—I mean inform his guests—that all—that everything's under control."

"Tim!" Like a slap the low command stemmed the confusion pouring like a broken recitation from the boy. When he grew quiet and ceased to fidget under the older man's riveting gaze, Gabe suggested, "Suppose you tell me what Mr. Butler says is under control."

"The fire."

"What fire?" Gabe asked patiently.

"The chimney. The fire truck's on its way. Of course," he added hastily, "it's just a precaution."

On the heels of Tim's assurance a second roar shook the veranda. The ash thickened to a gray haze and cinders that blazed fell on wet grass. Hundreds of tiny columns of smoke swirled toward the blackened cloud that hovered low over roof-tops. Murky and oppressive, unable to rise through the moisture-laden air, the smoke lay like a blanket over them.

"Tim," Gabe said coolly, "you'd better get on with your errand. Some of the guests might be frightened."

The last of his words were nearly lost in the keening wail of a siren, and the boy scurried reluctantly away. As it took the last sharp curve and passed the tall hedges that flanked the drive, an electric blue fire engine came into view. A burly man hunched over the wheel, dwarfing the cab, and men dressed in bright yellow rain garb clung to the sides. The engine had hardly skidded to a halt before they leapt to the ground.

"Oh, wow! This one's a lulu," a grave-faced fireman declared as he peered up at the roof covered in steaming debris that still belched from the massive chimney.

"Our Saturday excitement."

"Yeah, sure. Where's Caroline?"

"Here."

"You okay?"

"Right as rain."

"Speaking of rain, we're lucky we had some today."

"Precious little, but it will help."

As he listened to this exchange Gabe saw that beneath the loose concealing lines of their slickers most were lean and lanky. The exceptions were the driver and two others, neither of whom looked large or strong enough to manage the hoses. Gabe's interest focused lightly on the smaller of the two. Beneath the tilted helmet only the nape of a slender neck was visible, the skin smooth and creamy, a down of red brushing over it. His eyes narrowed thoughtfully before his attention was drawn to a commotion at the engine.

In deference to his bulk, the driver clambered slowly from its cab, barking a stream of unnecessary orders. "Butch," he bellowed to a tall man deftly unrolling a flat hose from its reel. "Get that line off the truck and unroll it."

"Yes, sir," Butch answered calmly, without looking up.

"Georgie Lee, you hook us into the hydrant and be quick about it. We don't have time to burn." A chuckle at his own pun set the fat around his middle in motion and Gabe was reminded of a good-natured bear.

"You've got it, Hiram." The cotton-haired man known as Georgie Lee, unperturbed at the tardy command, gave the connection one last turn with a heavy wrench.

"Who's up top?" Hiram's voice rose over the din of the fire that had settled to the sustained roar of a maniacal freight train.

"Caroline's on the way," Butch answered.

"Have to be extra careful today. Slate's like glass, particularly after rain." The huge man had a knack for stating the obvious.

"She knows that."

"Might not be a bad idea if Riley went up too." Hiram heaved his huge body about. "Riley! Where's Riley?"

"On the fire escape, Chief."

"Then tell him to go up and help."

"Yessir," Butch answered as he glanced at Riley, whose feet were clearing the gutter of the roof that sloped low before rising to a steep peak over the second story.

Gabe watched with growing admiration. They were volunteers, but they worked with split-second timing, always a step ahead of their chief. Descending to the flagstone walk, he found a better vantage point away from the gathering crowd.

The hoses that writhed and coiled from the force of the pumping water was turned on the smoldering lawn. Arching streams played over the gaily striped awning of a garden café. Torrents poured from the roof, washing away each new ember.

"That's enough up here for now." The call, clear and strong if a little husky, came from over Gabe's head.

As he looked up he caught a glimpse of an oval face and a pointed chin as determined as it was feminine. Before he could see more she spun and, unhampered by the long slicker, scrambled to the ridge of the roof. With an impatient gesture to push back her helmet that threatened blindness, she bent to check the copper gutter edging the slate.

It was, Gabe knew, a sensible division of labor. A volunteer too small to man the hoses was likely to be fleet of foot and agile and, logically, the better choice for the slippery roof. Logical, yes, Even practical. Then why did he feel a growing sense of dread?

"Why so much concern about the roof?" Gabe asked a passing fireman. "Slate can't burn."

"The inn's old," the man answered as he bent to tug the waterline to a new position. "Some of the tiles could be cracked or missing. The fire could penetrate there."

"No metal underlining?"

"Sure, but parts of it could have pulled away with a tile. One cinder in the right spot and the whole place would go up like so much tinder. Caroline's checking for bad patches so we can hose them down."

"Scrabbling around on slick slate can't be easy."

"Naw, but she'll be okay. Makes it look like kid's work."

"More slack here, Calvin," the chief interrupted.

"'Scuse me—" Calvin grinned at Gabe "—I'd best get a move on before Hiram gets a mite perturbed."

"Sorry, didn't mean to be a hindrance," Gabe said.

"It's all right, except Hiram does like to boss."

"I noticed." Gabe chuckled and stepped aside as Calvin shouldered the fat, snakelike hose. Then his attention was drawn again to the roof.

"Hiram," Caroline called, "the smoke's thinned out enough that I can check the chimney. Must be burned slick as a whistle. Shiloh won't need the chimney sweep this year. At least not for the kitchen chimney."

"Be careful up there, Donovan. Don't you go getting cocky now." Hiram squinted up at the face above.

"Wouldn't dare. I've got responsibilities, you know."

"Maybe you'd better let Riley do it."

"I can manage." In the shade of the helmet's brim and beneath the soot and grime, all that was visible was the sudden flash of a bright smile. With a jaunty, one-fingered salute she turned, moving like a yellow shadow over the slate. The heavy rubber soles of her waterproof boots seemed to grasp the surface like suction cups. Nimbly she balanced at the crest of the roof, then skipped over the ridge as surely as a tight-rope walker. Her hat slipped again over her eyes and an irritated swipe shoved it away.

A mass of red curls escaped from beneath it, tumbling over a broad, patrician forehead like a veil of fire. Gabe's suspicions were confirmed. Beneath the soot and grime, graceful and husky voiced Caroline Donovan was as beautiful as she was efficient.

"Trouble with your helmet, lady?" Riley asked.

"Can't adjust the strap. The buckle broke."

"You should have replaced it," he said grimly. "Hiram keeps some in the truck."

"I know, I won't be so careless next time." She smiled her thanks for his concern, then rose on tiptoe to examine the chimney. "I think there are still deposits on the left side of the firebrick. Shiloh just might need that sweep after all."

"Let me look, Shortstuff. I'm taller than the chimney."

"Bragging, Riley?"

"Now would I do that?"

"Without a doubt."

"You're right," Riley agreed with a laugh.

Gabe watched as Riley slipped and slithered to join her. When he reached the ridge he stood, teetered for a moment, then regained his balance. Suddenly his foot slipped. Like a windmill his arms flailed and his body swayed. Caroline grabbed him and for her trouble took a blow to the stomach that bent her double. She lost her footing, her shoulder crashed into the chimney, and her fingers clawed at it as she pitched forward.

"Heads up!" Her breathless voice shouted in warning as she skidded uncontrollably down the tiles. Fingers dug futilely into the shallow joints between the slate serving, only to slow her slide. Nothing could stop her fall.

"Caroline!" Riley's cry shattered the stillness as he righted himself and clutched the chimney in a frantic embrace.

The silence of horror hung over paralyzed spectators. But for her warning for those below and Riley's anguish, there had been no sound from the roof. Caroline fought a silent battle and only Gabe moved, a muttered prayer on his lips. His racing steps brought him to the base of the inn's foundation at the desperate instant Caroline's last clawing grasp found nothing to hold on to. He had no time to brace himself for her fall. The impact of her hurtling body buckled his knees, driving the breath from his body. For a stunned moment he clutched at her fighting to draw oxygen back to his laboring lungs. In harsh, gasps his breath returned and he placed his scrutiny on Caroline.

He'd known the slicker was bulky yet he was startled at the slightness of the form he held. The helmet, as was its habit, had slipped down until it rested against her chin. Gabe could see nothing but soot-streaked yellow from the hat brim to the black tips of her boots. Lowering her to the grass he slipped the loose strap free and pushed the helmet away. As it tumbled from the tousled hair Gabe found himself staring into the most beautiful gray eyes he'd ever seen.

"Nice catch," she managed as she struggled to fill her own lungs.

"My pleasure," he said. "But I hope not too frequently."

"Me too." Her laugh quivered and faded as her air-starved lungs failed her.

The laugh struck a nerve. Gabe was suddenly blazingly angry, his hand closed in a tight grip over her shoulder. "Dammit, woman! How can you laugh? You might have been killed! Don't you have enough sense to be afraid?"

"I was petrified," she answered quietly. "I know what could have happened if it hadn't been my lucky day."

"Your 'lucky day'?" His voice was thick with sarcasm. "Only a card-carrying lunatic would see any luck in this."

"You were here," she said simply, and Gabe discovered her lilting voice and the level gaze disrupted his breathing as violently as the force of her fall.

"Yes," he managed at last. "I was here." His anger faded as quickly as it had come. He'd expected tears and trembling and instead found cool calm touched with a hint of humor. He understood now. The banter was her way of dealing with the fear. He'd known men who laughed in the face of danger, perhaps he'd even done it himself. But a woman? What other surprises did she hold for him?

Tearing himself away from her mesmerizing gaze, his eyes trailed over her. The mass of red curls that defied the crush of the hat were springing back into a fiery halo about her head. The sweep of her forehead was high and unlined, the pert nose dusted with almost invisible freckles. A dimple marked one cheek and her full lips were curved in the beginning of a smile. The body that had pressed so briefly against his had been soft and yielding. Still, it was the eyes that enchanted. Red from smoke, with dark smudges of soot circling them, he saw serenity in their depths.

Gabe found himself captivated by that serenity. Something stirred inside him. The jaded veneer that encased him slowly slipped away, and long-forgotten hopes and dreams were laid bare. It was insanity, but the hunger for those dreams couldn't he denied. Madness, too, was the desire that quickened suddenly, hot and heavy in him. Irrational, illogical, insane, undeniable, stranger that she was, Caroline Donovan stirred him.

"Caroline!" Riley pushed his way frantically through the silent, watching crowd. Kneeling by Gabe, he hovered anxiously over her. "Are you hurt?"

"I'm fine, Riley," she assured him as she turned slowly from Gabe. "All I have to show for my great slide are some scratches."

"Don't joke. I almost killed you."

"Hey—" Caroline clasped Riley's clenched fist in her battered hands "—you know better than that. It could have been either of us. I'm fine, so forget it."

"Then if you're okay, and you can get this gentleman to let you up, I suggest we get on with our fire fighting." Hiram spoke as he moved like a tank through the curious bystanders. With a callused hand he ruffled her curls, then winked at Gabe who saw the hidden concern. "We owe you one, mister."

"The name's Jackson. Gabe Jackson," Gabe answered without looking away from Caroline. Reluctantly he lifted her to her feet, and keeping his arm about her shoulders, he steadied her. Her hair barely brushed his chin, and a drift of honeysuckle tantalized him and then was gone. He realized with a start that she still watched him.

"You have a nice name." Her quiet comment was muffled by the roar of Hiram's next command. Watchers and volunteers alike scurried to do his bidding.

"My mother thought so. She had a penchant for angels." They were alone now. The knowledge registered somewhere in the far recesses of Gabe's mind, and he fought the impulse to draw her back into his arms.

"The archangel." She nodded, then smiled up at him. "Don't you like your name, Gabriel Jackson?"

He didn't wince as he usually did. Instead he murmured, "The way you say it, I do."

"How do I say it?" One brow arched up in question and Gabe was bewitched.

"Softly. You say my name softly." His head tipped near, his breath stirred against her hair, his gaze touched her lips like a caress. He had a fleeting impression of astonishment widening the dark-fringed eyes. He whispered as much to himself as to her, "I've never kissed a fireman before."

A giggle—it could be called nothing else—bubbled from her throat in a happy, infectious sound. Gabe stopped cold. He drew an irritated breath, then a slow, answering smile touched his lips as he moved away. Gazes met, clung, challenged.

"Laugh, lovely lady. I can wait." He brushed a sooty ash from her cheek. He'd never felt like this and he'd rushed her, but he wouldn't again. "I can wait, but I promise you, for us there will be kisses with the laughter."

Caroline's smile faltered, her brow puckered in a frown. "I'm afraid you've made a mistake: my gratitude doesn't extend to what you seem to want."

"No mistake," he murmured. "And it's not gratitude I want."

"Caroline!" Gabe moved away unhurriedly as Hiram's gruff grumble intruded. "If you can tear yourself away from Mr. Jackson, we could use your help."

"Sure, Hiram. Duty calls." Her frown disappeared, his promise put aside but not forgotten. Her voice grew huskier. "Thank you, Gabe Jackson."

"Are you really all right?" he asked.

"Perfectly, and because of you." She flashed him a smile and turned away.

"Wait." His hand on her arm stopped her. "Your hands, your palms at least—you will get them seen to, won't you?"

"There's no need."

"You should get treatment," Gabe persisted.

"What needs to be done about some scratches? They don't need stitches."

"The slate's filthy. Maybe you need an injection."

"Nope. I'm up-to-date on everything. Even tetanus. So, I'd say I'm pretty well covered."

"Are you never serious?" Gabe remembered how she'd shrugged aside Riley's concern.

"What's there to be serious about? This is nothing, it hardly even bled. But if it'll make you and Riley feel better, I'll see the doc first thing after we finish here. Satisfied?"

Gabe couldn't resist chuckling at the exasperated look she gave him. He had no idea how old she might be, but at the moment she looked barely sixteen. She gave him her half salute and jogged away.

"Hey," he called after her, "when can I see you?"

"I'll be around. You can't miss me."

"Where are you going now?"

"Back on the roof."

"You can't go back up there."

"I can't?"

"No, it's slick."

"So I found out." She had reached the first step of the fire escape. Taking them two at a time she was at the rim of the roof in seconds, and in a few more she was walking the ridgepole of a gable.

The only reminders of the fire were the lingering smell of smoke and the pockmarks of scorched grass that scored the trampled lawn. Gabe lounged against a post at the veranda's edge, his gaze trained on the sun that had already dipped behind the mountains, his thoughts of serene gray eyes.

Caroline. What a contradiction she was. The improbable occupation should have been his first warning, the gleaming mass of curls that matched her fiery spirit his second. But how could he have known that when he held her in his arms he would find himself bewitched and aching with desire.

"Ridiculous," he scoffed. "You've wined and dined women all over the world. They've all been the same. So will Caroline." Before the words were past his lips he remembered the feel of her body and knew he lied.

He kicked a cinder from the floor, then bent to right the chair he'd overturned earlier. His hat lay nearby—

as he scooped it up the scent of scorched fabric was strong. On closer inspection he saw it was peppered with countless pinhole burns and one that would accommodate a gold ball.

"Looks more like a sieve than a hat," he grumbled, sinking into the chair. "Guess it will do until it rains."

With the hat cocked at a raffish angle and his feet again propped one over the other on the banister, Gabe let his mind drift back through the years. As a civil engineer, his life had been one construction site and one Third World country after another until they had become a jumbled blur. He'd lived with danger for so long it seemed the natural order of things. Freedom and simplicity had been smothered by the clandestine and exotic—until the King Abdul Aziz International Airport in Saudi Arabia, and a bullet meant for some little-known sheik. The snipers didn't care who else they shot and he'd been one of the lucky ones. The only reminder Gabe carried from that day of slaughter was a furrow in his skull, persistent headaches and sporadic dizziness.

Vertigo and the lure of peace had brought him back to Stonebridge. Gabe smiled, remembering Sam Danton's startled expression when he'd finally agreed to a period of rest. Sam, friend as well as physician, had been adamant, insisting Gabe take time away from the heat of the desert and from the pressures of his work. He'd ignored any protestations of recovery. In the midst of their most heated argument Sam had fixed him with a pragmatic stare and commented dryly that Gabe was alive only because he was so hardheaded. Not even he could expect to sacrifice a sliver of skull and suffer no consequences. Still Gabe argued.

"No," Sam had said. "Our work's too sensitive, too crucial for a man whose judgment might be distorted by pain. But more than that, I can't allow a man I love like a brother to risk his life. The matter's settled. Clearance denied." With that, Gabe had capitulated.

"Mr. Jackson." Hurrying footsteps halted at Gabe's side. "Is there anything you need before I leave?"

He put aside his interrupted memories, tipped the hat back from his eyes and smiled up at Tim. "I'm fine. Don't need a thing."

"Yes, sir. Have a good evening."

"Good night." The boy had reached the last step when Gabe called after him. "Tim."

"Sir?"

"Do you know the fireman called Caroline?"

"Sure. Everybody knows Caroline."

"How old is she?"

"I don't know, pretty old I guess. She's got a kid named Pete who's the same age as my sister."

"Then she's married."

"Gosh, no. She's only thirteen. Mom won't even let her date yet." A blush rushed to his young face as he realized his blunder. "Oh. You meant is Caroline married."

"Never mind, you answered my question." Gabe felt the weight of fatigue and the first flickering of a headache.

"But I didn't. I mean she's not. Married, I mean." Tim's words tumbled over themselves as he hastened to correct the misunderstanding. "Not anymore, at least."

"Divorced?" Relief threaded through Gabe.

"No, sir, a widow. Her husband was declared MIA, then four years ago she found out he'd died."

"And now?" Gabe hesitated. He was prying, but he had to know. "Is there a man in her life now?"

"I don't know for sure, but I don't think so. I heard my Aunt Julie telling my mom the other day that fourteen years was long enough for Caroline to devote to Mark Donovan."

"Mark was her husband?"

"Yes, sir."

"And your Aunt Julie?"

"Julie Townsend, the hostess here."

"Ahh yes." Gabe nodded. "She knew both of them?"

"Yes, sir. Mark only lived here for a little while, but Julie and Caroline grew up together." Tim scuffed a foot against the rough edge of a step and glanced at his watch. "Is there anything else?"

"No. I've kept you long enough. Have a good evening."

"Thanks, Mr. Jackson. See you tomorrow."

Tim had been gone for quite some time before Gabe stirred from his reverie. His unexpected shout of laughter resounded through the deserted veranda as he recalled the irony of Sam's parting words. "No work, no wine, no women, no song. Absolutely no excitement until you've been free of headaches for six months. But with you stuck in those desolate hills I won't worry about excitement."

"Ah, Sam," Gabe mused, "what would you say if you knew I'd met a woman more exciting than all the exotic jobs and countries in the world?"

The exhilaration he'd once known as he faced each new challenge had been reborn. What this sooty-faced enchantress stirred in his heart was too fragile to be understood. But whatever it was, he knew instinctively that Caroline was a challenge and a risk worth taking. In a lighthearted impulse he snatched the tattered hat from his head and sailed it over the railing. Rolling end over end it came to rest at the feet of a man who stepped out of the shadows.

In a graceful movement, Shiloh Butler, innkeeper extraordinaire, scooped the hat from the ground. For a long moment neither Gabe nor Shiloh moved. One dark-haired, dark-skinned man took the measure of the other. Tension crackled. Then grave features nearly hidden by the shadows were touched with a wry smile, and eyes as blue as Gabe's own glittered in the dim light.

"Hat in the ring, so to speak, Mr. Jackson?" Shiloh questioned in an oblique confirmation that Tim's interrogation had been overheard.

"So to speak, Mr. Butler," Gabe replied.

"I wish you luck."

"I suspect I'll need it."

"You will." Shiloh chuckled, then turned, and Gabe was alone.

Two

Gabe stepped from the shower as the bedside phone rang. His first impulse was to ignore it. Jet lag, the fire, the headache he'd tried to deny, had brought on a crushing fatigue. He firmly intended an early bath, a few minutes' reading and then sleep. The jangling command of the telephone was little reason to change his plans. As he dried his lean torso with a heavy towel, the ringing stopped.

Only three rings. Gabe waited. Nothing. Dismissing the intrusion with a flex of tired shoulders, he wrapped the towel about himself and tucked it tightly at the waist. Wrong number, he decided. Nobody knew he was here except Sam. Considering the hour, Gabe doubted that Sam had the time or the inclination to be calling.

After running a comb through his freshly washed hair, Gabe crossed to the rack that held his briefcase.

Riffling through it he extracted a thick sheaf of papers covered by lines, graphs and columns of numbers. "The way I feel, this should be better than a sleeping pill," he said to himself.

Slipping the towel from his waist and tossing it over a chair, he stepped to the bed, flipped back the covers and eased his weary body between the sheets. In a matter of minutes he was deep into facts, figures and projections for a future construction project.

Again the phone jangled. This time the ringing seemed louder and more annoying. Gabe frowned irritably and his eyes never left the folder as he fumbled with the receiver. Sam. It had to be Sam. Gabe lifted the instrument from its cradle, silencing it in midring.

"What's up, Sam?" He propped the receiver between chin and shoulder and turned a page.

"Since I'm not Sam, I don't know." A familiar low-voiced laugh flowed over him. "Perhaps I should hang up so you can find out."

"No! Wait!" The phone slipped from its spot beneath his chin, falling with a thud against the table. In his haste to catch it his elbow cracked the brass lamp with a force that sent it reeling against the wall. It tottered at the table's edge then toppled slowly over. Gabe's desperate lunge for it was a farce. His hand missed the lamp. Trapped by the tangle of covers, he sprawled full length over the floor in a snarl of cords and sheets. As a final indignity the lamp shade landed with ludicrous precision on his head.

"Dammit!" He tried to rise and was nearly strangled by a mesh of wires.

"Gabe!" The muffled words came from somewhere beneath the yards of heavy pleated muslin that wrapped his naked body like a mummy. His first grim exploration of the heap produced nothing.

"Gabe? Are you there?" Muted as it was, the voice was as unmistakable.

"Yes, dammit! I'm here. Where the hell are you?" Reciting every curse he knew in every language, he systematically searched for the receiver. "Aha!" He snatched it from its hiding place beyond his toes. "There you are."

With the dignity he could recover he said, "Gabe Jackson speaking."

"Yes, I should say you have been." Caroline chuckled. "You've got quite a vocabulary."

"Spectacular, isn't it?" Gabe could only agree. "I've been years acquiring it."

"I can believe that. I don't think I understood more than half of it."

"It's just as well you didn't."

"I can believe that too," she said as she laughed again. "What on earth were you doing?"

"You wouldn't believe it."

"Oh no?"

"No." He was emphatic.

"If you say so." Caroline abandoned the subject. "Hiram and the crew are down in the bar—we hoped you'd join us for a drink. I certainly owe you one."

"It's not a drink you owe me, Caroline." He paused a beat to let that register. "I'll be down as soon as I change."

There was silence at the other end, then the soft releasing of a breath. He could almost see her struggle to regain her composure. It came as no surprise when she spoke cheerfully, determined to ignore the allusion to the averted kiss. "No need for that. Come as you are. We're pretty casual here."

"I think I'd better change. I don't think you're quite ready for this."

"Exactly what are you wearing?"

"At the moment," he relented. "A curtain and a lamp shade."

"What?"

"There. What did I tell you? I knew you wouldn't believe me." Gabe's drawling self-pity brought a peal of laughter from Caroline. She was back on familiar ground.

"Oh, I believe you. I really do," she insisted. "I'm wondering if you need another drink."

"Haven't had the first one yet. I'm sober as a judge."

"Sure you are."

"I only fell off the bed. Who fell off the roof and dares to accuse *me* of tippling? That's gratitude?"

"Poor baby." Caroline was unsuccessful in hiding a giggle. It was a delightful sound, Gabe decided. "Never mind. Just come on down and I'll buy you that drink. Then maybe things will look better."

"Five minutes?"

"I'll be waiting."

Gabe was smiling with no trace of exhaustion as he unwound the cord that coiled snakelike about his arm. A quick search produced the rest of the telephone. The receiver was almost in its cradle when he heard Caroline's voice.

"Gabe."

"Yes." This time the phone rested firmly in the palm of his hand. One fiasco was more than enough.

"What color did you say the sheets were?"

"I didn't. But they're blue."

"Oh, I see. They match your eyes."

"Five minutes, Caroline."

"Sure." The broken connection silenced her laughter.

The curving stairs were broad; the gleaming handrail of polished oak. Thick, deep-pile carpet muffled Gabe's hurried footsteps. The steady beat of recorded music and the hum of voices greeted him. He looked up in midtask of coping with a button at his wrist, surprised to find the bar so completely occupied. A celebration was in progress.

He waited at the doorway, searching the crowded room. One by one he recognised the firemen—Georgie Lee, Riley, Hiram, Butch, some others he could match with no names—and Caroline.

As he watched, she tilted her head slowly and laughed. Her eyes crinkled, there was the sudden flash of white teeth. Her whole body seemed to move and a surprisingly deep guffaw filled the room. It was a lovely sound, full-bodied and hearty. Like Caroline herself, it was vibrant, charming.

Gabe knew then what hunger she stirred in him. She was the joy he'd lost; the laughter he'd forgotten. She was tiny, almost fragile, but like David and his Goliath she met life squarely with a happy ferocity. Would she bring that fierceness to her lovemaking? Would her passion burn like a fever? When it was spent, would there be serenity?

He wanted to know. He wanted to see her warm and flushed and heavy lidded with desire. He wanted the softness of her satin skin against his. He wanted to hear her low, shuddering cry of ecstasy. Lord, how he wanted her.

"You're mad. Stark, raving mad," he muttered and failed to notice the startled look on Julie Townsend's face as she approached, a look quickly replaced by a genuine smile.

Oblivious to those around him as well as Julie, Gabe cursed his stupidity in a low mutter. Instant attractions were for the young or the foolish, and at thirty-eight he was neither. Yet there it was. He wanted her. Maybe the Arab bullet had clipped more than a piece of his skull. Maybe he was just tired. Maybe Sam was more right than he knew to insist on this rest. Maybe tomorrow, after a good night's sleep, he'd see this more clearly. Yeah, maybe.

"A table, Mr. Jackson?" Julie stopped before him, a soft, full caftan swaying about her beautifully pregnant body, a sheaf of menus in her hand.

"What?" Gabe still seemed not to see her as he climbed from the depths of his thoughts.

"A table?" Julie repeated patiently. Gabe Jackson had come into the dining room or bar several times in the short course of his stay and each time he'd been pleasant. Hesitantly she asked, "Is something wrong?"

"No, Julie, I just...never mind." Turning back, hardly bothering to apologize as he jostled a new arrival, he strode to the door.

"Gabe!" Caroline's voice stopped him in midstride. He faced her almost reluctantly.

"Four and a half minutes. Even better than you promised." She came to him with both hands outstretched in welcome. Her skin was warm, her grasp firm as she took his hands in hers. A bandage on one palm was soft like cotton against his. "Come join us. We want you to be a part of our celebration. It's something we do after a successful call."

"Today was a successful call?"

"Definitely. No real property damage, no injury."

"Except very nearly you." A muscle danced in his jaw as he relived the silent horror of her slide down steep slate.

"That's the point. It wasn't me, thanks to you." She dropped one of his hands but gripped the other tighter. "Gabe was supposed to join us, Julie. He must have failed to recognize us without our rain garb."

Julie nodded with smothered amazement at the sight of Caroline, forever the widow, and Mr. Jackson.

With a brilliant smile Caroline tugged and Gabe followed. Arab bullet or not, he knew he'd follow her anywhere. At least until he'd unraveled the mystery of this attraction and understood why her touch was a soothing balm for hurts long buried; until he'd figured out why this woman could probe the depths of his soul with only a smile. Until then, he would stay and he would follow. Then he'd go.

"Here. This place has been reserved especially for you." She waited at his side as he stood by the chair she indicated. A look of pleased expectation glittered in her eyes, like a child with a special secret. Gabe cast a puzzled glance down the long table, then slipped into the seat.

"Are you up to something?" he asked her.

"Not me. Hiram has something to say."

On cue Hiram rose from his seat and tapped his glass with a spoon. "If you'll give me your attention, we'll get on with this, and I promise to be brief."

Rocking back on his heels, he waited good-naturedly for the laughter to subside. "Caroline, why don't you sit down."

Gabe pulled out the chair by his side and Caroline slid into it. He touched her shoulder in a light caress and turned back to the chief.

"Now then, Mr. Jackson," Hiram said. "You've been asked to take part in a very private party. This is a special time when the men and women of Stonebridge One-0-Five lift a glass and say a word of thanks. To make you legal, you're now an honorary member. Where is it, Georgie?"

"Got it right here, Chief." From beneath the table, Georgie produced a huge box that was passed from one fireman to another until it sat before Gabe.

"Caroline, why don't you do the honors?" Hiram suggested.

She flipped the top off the box and lifted from its wrapping a gleaming fire hat. Holding it before her she waited for Hiram to continue.

"In appreciation of your quick thinking and fast action this afternoon, we proclaim you to be a member of One-0-Five, with all the benefits it entails. Put his hat on, Caroline."

Darkness enveloped Gabe as the hat slipped over his head, then came to rest on the bridge of his nose. Nobody moved or spoke. Then one reluctant chuckle followed another, until together they became a roar. Slapping knees and wiping tears from their cheeks, the taciturn men of Stonebridge laughed.

"Well," Caroline offered at last in a strained voice, "at least it's better than a lamp shade."

With one finger against the brim, Gabe slowly pushed the hat back to his forehead. "You think so?"

"Except it doesn't match your eyes."

"How can you tell?" Deliberately he let the hat fall back over his face.

"Memory," she retorted and swept the hat from his head, replacing it in the box. "Let's just put it here before you get another broken nose."

"You've noticed."

"Your broken nose?"

"My eyes."

"You have two. Blue. On either side of your nose."

"You like them," Gabe said confidently.

Caroline flushed, tried to look away and couldn't. "I usually like for people to have eyes," she managed. "It completes their faces."

"Speech! Speech!" Heavy mugs banged in cadence.

Gabe's gaze held Caroline's, refusing to release it. "Shall we postpone this discussion until later?"

"Speech! Speech!" The chant escalated.

"Your public commands." Caroline was evasive, excited and frightened by the intimacy woven like silk through the invitation.

"Later?"

"Speech! Speech!" The uproar was deafening.

"You'd better make that speech before Shiloh has to replenish his supply of glasses."

"Later?" Gabe folded his arms across his chest stubbornly. He didn't care how many glasses Shiloh lost.

"All right! Dinner! Soon." Her resistance melted, but she knew it had very little to do with concern for Shiloh's glassware. This man with the cold eyes that transformed into sparkling sapphires when he laughed intrigued her. The intimate challenge that simmered just beneath the surface attracted her even as it disturbed.

Gabe pushed back his chair and stood. When the pounding and the calls quieted he looked from one face to the next. These were strong, insular men, protective of home and custom. They did not easily accept strangers. Yet, tonight they had. It was a measure of their affection for Caroline. They'd shown him how much she meant to them.

"Thank you. Inadequate words to express my understanding of what this represents." He rested his hand on the hatbox. "But I do understand." He watched as gazes turned toward Caroline. It was in their faces, he could read it. In one way or another, every man at the table loved her—as father, brother, companion, friend. Could there be a lover among them?

She watched him raptly, completely unaware of what passed between the men. In her face was innocence. Gabe was almost certain Caroline had no lover. He cleared the unexpected tightness from his throat and addressed the men: "I accept this in the spirit in which it's given, but we all know there's not a man in this room who wouldn't have done the same."

"A toast." Hiram scraped back his chair and stood with his glass lifted. "To Caroline. The best little fire fighter Stonebridge ever had."

"Hear! Hear!" They were on their feet. Glasses touched, were upended, drained.

Caroline's eyes grew suspiciously bright. As empty glasses thumped in unison on the table, she rose, lifting her own. "My turn. To old friends, the best anyone could have." She turned to Gabe. "And to new friends."

There was a stillness about the men as Caroline drained her glass and set it just as vigorously on the table.

"Harrumph!" Hiram coughed noisily and wiped his cheeks with a huge handkerchief. "Now that this is all settled, let's have some music. Caroline, did you bring your guitar?"

"I thought I'd just listen." She wagged the bandaged hand.

"All right. You and Mr. Jackson sit tight and enjoy."

Instruments appeared. Georgie had a trumpet, Calvin a fiddle, Butch a set of drums, and Riley took a seat at the piano. Hiram tuned a banjo, diminished by the large hands that held it tenderly. There were other instruments and other players and soon the room was alive with sound. Gabe expected that they would play country music, and they did—followed by Gershwin and Bacharach. Then Riley played a short excerpt Gabe could have sworn was a bastardized Grieg concerto.

He glanced away from the group and found that Caroline watched him. The look on her face told him she'd enjoyed his astonishment. Perhaps he'd underestimated these people, but he was learning. Riley chose that moment to begin the slow, easy rhythm of a love song.

"Shall we?" Gabe took her hand carefully in his.

"I'd be delighted."

Together they rose and Caroline stepped into his arms. There was no dance floor, but they moved along the scattered tables. Beyond the massive bar with its glitter of crystal there was only the light from the flickering lamps at each table. As they drifted into the shadows he drew her closer.

Gabe was a bit over average height, not huge. The aura of size that clung to him was enhanced by the heavy muscle of shoulders and chest. Yet as Caroline's small body nestled into his he was a giant, massive and towering. Soft curls that brushed the angular jut of his jaw caught the light and gleamed like fire. There was again the haunting fragrance of honeysuckle. Delightful, like Caroline herself. "Your fragrance suits you."

"What?" Caroline missed a step and narrowly missed planting her heel on his instep.

"You truly are honeysuckle."

"I am?" She resumed the rhythm but in the dim light he could see the questioning expression on her upturned face.

"Honeysuckle symbolizes the bond of love. You bind us to you with love of one sort or another."

"Are you sure you're sober? You're being fanciful, you know."

"Sober, yes. Fanciful, no. Look at them."

She followed the direction of his nod. Her friends, the people who shared her life, were sharing their music.

"Do you love them?" Gabe asked softly.

"Yes. I do."

"Tonight they've shown you how they feel about you."

"I know." Tears glittered before the dark sweep of lashes hid them. As quickly as they came, they were gone. She looked into his face curiously. "Tell me more about flowers."

"No mystery. Every flower has a meaning."

"How strange."

"That people who love flowers give them significance? I don't think so."

"No, not that. It's strange coming from you."

"When I was very young my grandmother taught me."

"Her philosophy of flowers became yours."

"In a way I suppose it did." He guided her by the bandsmen and began to circle the room again.

"Where do you make your home?" Caroline asked suddenly.

"I've had no home in a long time, but I spent my childhood in Charleston."

"The Charleston drawl is missing."

"It was lost in the course of my work, honed away a little more in each new country."

"Have there been many countries?"

"A few." The answer was terse and, Caroline suspected, an understatement.

"Not always peaceful," she suggested as her eyes flashed to the thick hair at his temple where she'd glimpsed a scar.

"Not always." His jaw was rigid, his lips tightened into a thin line. Caroline realized she'd touched on painful memories.

"So—" she smiled her brightest and steered the conversation to a lighter vein "—you lost an accent and gained a vocabulary."

"Something like that." Gabe relaxed.

"Strange," she murmured. "You've traveled the world, yet you're contented, for now, in a village in the hills. You've lived with danger but speak of flowers and bonds of love. You're an intriguing man, Gabe Jackson."

"I hope so. I truly hope so."

The tempo of the music changed, grew softer, slower. He wrapped both arms about Caroline and held her closer. Caroline's head leaned forward, her cheek rested against his chest. Gabe was reminded again of how fragile she was. Holding her was like holding a flower.

One song flowed into another. If the musicians tired they gave no indication. They played and watched, wondering if Caroline was at last breaking from the chrysalis of a solitary life.

"Well! Music and dancin.'" A raucous voice from the bar grated across the strains. "Sounds like a funeral. Give the band a dollar, Harry, and see if they can liven up the place."

Gabe groaned and Caroline lifted her head from his shoulder, taking with her a memory of his cologne. Like Gabe it was masculine and clean, a little spicy. It evoked thoughts of quiet evenings, good books, old velvet and jeans. And love hidden in every look.

"Would you prefer to sit this next one out? I suspect it'll be wild." His breath was like a kiss against her hair.

"What?" Caroline stared up at him blankly. Old velvet and jeans? Where on earth did that come from? Gabe was nothing like that. He was excitement and danger, a traveler. Here today, gone tomorrow. No quiet evenings for him. Nor love in every look.

"Caroline?" He touched her cheek and she discovered she and Gabe were no longer dancing.

"Oh," she stammered. "I don't think I'm in the mood for more dancing."

Gabe led her back to their table. Once they were seated the band struck up a rousing tone. Hiram's huge fingers moved over the strings of his banjo faster than the eye could comprehend. Had Gabe doubted his talent, he could no longer.

"Perhaps I should be glad of this." He lifted her injured hand from the table and cradled it in his.

"You should?"

"Without it you'd be up there playing with them and we wouldn't have danced. We dance well together."

"I'd almost forgotten how. It's been a long time. Mark and I—" She stopped short, catching her lip between her teeth.

"I know about Mark, Caroline," Gabe said gently. "Tim told me."

"You questioned Tim about Mark?"

"About you. I wanted to know everything there is to know about you. The past and now."

"Why, Gabe?" She looked steadily at him with no hint of a smile.

"Caroline." The deep voice and the fond touch of a tanned hand at her shoulder forestalled Gabe's answer.

"Shiloh!" Caroline surged from her seat into the embrace of Shiloh Butler.

"Your hand's bandaged." The words were an accusation, the tone caring. Shiloh's hand buried in the mass of curls pressed against his chest. The gentleness of the gesture clashed with his saturnine looks. He was dark, lean and powerfully built. His features were taut and hard, cast into an expression of cruelty by the slash of a scar through the lid and corner of his left eye and cheek. The startling blue of his gaze was cold and piercing, until he looked at Caroline. The transformation was shocking: there was naked warmth and caring that he didn't bother to hide. Now a frown of stark worry creased his face. That he had totally ignored Gabe was a revelation. "Is it bad?"

"Just a scratch. I don't know why everyone's making such a fuss over it." Caroline leaned back in his arms. "When did you get back?"

"Late last night. I meant to call you earlier today, but a little matter of a chimney fire took care of that." Shiloh tugged a curl. "I was told you did a swan dive off the roof." His tone was playful and teasing now, but to Gabe, perceptive and watchful, Shiloh Butler was deeply concerned.

"I don't think it qualified as a swan dive," Caroline laughed. "Too clumsy."

"It's no laughing matter, Caroline. It's bothered me for a long time that it's always you who ends up on the roof," Shiloh said in a tight voice.

"But nothing's ever happened. At least not until today," she protested.

"That's just the point—" Shiloh was not to be swayed "—today it did!"

"For heaven's sake, Shiloh! You'd think I was twelve instead of thirty-two." A look of exasperation crossed her features as she stepped away from him. "I've told you, nothing really happened. Thanks to Gabe. Oh—" she turned toward Gabe who stood now, then back to Shiloh "—this is—"

"We've met, briefly," Shiloh interrupted her introduction tersely.

"Gabe was there at the crucial point of my dive."

"I heard. We're in your debt, Jackson." Shiloh offered his hand.

"My pleasure," Gabe said as strong grips met. Beneath the trappings of cordiality no expression touched the face of either man. Their gazes challenged and probed, and neither faltered.

"Ho! Shiloh," Hiram laid aside his banjo and wiped his face with his handkerchief. "Missed you today."

"Sorry." Shiloh loosened his hand and turned away. "By the time I calmed things in the kitchen you had the rest under control. Good job."

"All in a day's work." Hiram waved a deprecating hand. "Best get the chimney cleaned."

"I intend to." Shiloh turned again to Caroline.

"What about your eye? Did the smoke bother it?" Caroline skimmed her fingers over his temple near the scar. The odd moment between Shiloh and Gabe had passed so quickly she would've doubted it had she not sensed their cautious restraint.

"Some irritation, that's all," Shiloh assured her.

"Maybe you should wear a patch to protect it," she teased in an effort to ease the tension. "It would make you seem mysterious and aloof, and very wicked."

"Me?" He laughed. The kiss he dropped onto her forehead was as quick and light as his tone. If he felt the weight of Gabe's speculative stare, he ignored it.

"Yes. You," Caroline said. "Now, if you gentlemen will have a seat, I'll draw you both a beer."

Silence hovered thickly after Caroline had gone. Gabe leaned indolently in his chair, his body relaxed, a smile pasted on his lips. The rhythmic beat of his fingers at the table's edge was at odds with his icy regard of the man across the table. Shiloh Butler was a renegade. Gabe had sensed it the night he arrived, encountering the lean stranger at the front desk—a jarring note among the tranquil. The less-than-informative conversation by the veranda had only reinforced first impressions. The man was a maverick beyond the trappings of convention. Not the kind to be found happily trusting his life and fortune to the running of a small-town inn.

"Have you lived here long, Mr. Butler?" The band was playing a soft melody, but it was cover enough that Gabe's quiet question was heard only by the one he intended.

"A while." Shiloh slid a matchbook end over end through his fingers. Graceful, hypnotic, distracting and calculated.

The noncommittal answer was no surprise. It was the answer Gabe would have given himself. He probed again: "One doesn't usually find your type in a place like this."

"And what type is that?" The matchbook slipped through long, tapered fingers.

The question needed no answer. Gabe understood as well as Shiloh. It was time to get to the point. "What's your interest here?"

"The same as yours, I would imagine," Shiloh drawled.

"Caroline?"

Shiloh nodded. The matchbook continued to move.

"Hat in the ring, so to speak, Mr. Butler?"

"No." The matchbook was still. Drumming fingers stopped. They watched the flame-haired woman move through the crowd with mugs raised high. Once again gazes as piercing as honed steel met. "I'm a friend, no more," Shiloh murmured. "An interested observer."

"Here you go." Caroline thumped the mugs down before them laughing when, in her exuberance, the white foamy head sloshed over the rim. "Sorry. I'll get a cloth."

"No." Shiloh's fingers circled her wrist. "A little spilled beer won't hurt anything. Stay."

Caroline looked from one to the other. She'd left them alone, hoping in her absence they would warm to each other, but their enmity was almost palpable. "Is something wrong?"

"Of course not," Shiloh assured her. "Mr. Jackson and I were just getting acquainted."

"Gabe?" She sat stiffly on the edge of the seat Shiloh had drawn out for her.

"Relax, Caroline. Mr. Butler was telling me how things are." He gave her his most charming smile and leaned back into his chair with careful ease. If Shiloh Butler called himself friend, then friend he would be. A dangerous friend if anyone should hurt Caroline.

Gabe had no intention of hurting her, yet he admired and respected the protective interest he'd witnessed. Lifting his glass and nodding, he acknowledged Shiloh's subtle warning. "To friends," he said softly, "and interested observers." He drank once, sparingly, and stood. He touched Caroline's cheek, his fingers lingering. She was warm, a little flushed, and puzzled. "Mr. Butler will explain," he said. "It's been a long day. Good night, Caroline."

He heard the low rush of her questions and Shiloh's gruff rumble as he crossed the room. Yes, Mr. Butler, explain what just passed between us, if you can. Gabe almost chuckled aloud as he stepped through the door.

Three

___

Gabe paused at a small footbridge arching over a shallow creek. It was one of three streams, born in the Blue Ridge Mountains, that twisted through the low hills to converge, becoming Stoney River. Stones from the aptly named river had been dragged from its bed to build another bridge. The huge, old bridge that had eventually given its name to the settlement that had grown up around it.

With none of the magnitude of mountain or shore, the land here offered a restful sense of space and balance. This restfulness, and the antiquity that survived in the tiny hamlet of Stonebridge, was the reason Gabe's automobile remained at the inn while he had strolled the quiet street that drowsed in the setting sun.

"Six o'clock. It's time," Gabe said aloud. The week had been interminable as he waited for Caroline's call. He'd had only her vague promise of dinner the night of the fire, and his own belief that her word was binding. When he'd begun to doubt, his phone had rung in the dark of night, the whispered invitation sweeping the cobwebs of sleep from his mind.

This was the appointed time, today the appointed day. Gabe stepped onto the weathered boards. His footsteps were muffled by the tumbling water and the world seemed suspended in stillness. Beyond the bridge a flagstone path wound through a small garden and over a neatly kept lawn. The house, of rough stone, glass and silvered oak, blended unpretentiously into its wooded surroundings. A brass knocker turned green by time was affixed squarely in the center of a paneled door. With one last appreciation for architect and builder, Gabe lifted the heavy ring and tapped.

There was no answer. He rapped again with as little response. The doorbell gave the appearance of disuse—the button was missing, but the mechanism seemed intact. From his pocket Gabe took a small knife and inserted its point into the empty socket. He was rewarded by three short chimes. He rang the bell twice more.

Get the hell away from that door!

The raucous shout was shrill and cutting, and decidedly not Caroline's. Gabe's eyes, steady and watchful, narrowed slightly. As always with the unexpected, he waited.

Go 'way! Go 'way!

This time the voice was weak and trembling. The surprise that held Gabe immobile eased and a wry expression crossed his face. Had he blundered into the lair of some fierce recluse? Unlikely, with Caroline's simple directions, yet he'd obviously made a mistake.

"Look," he called through the door, "sorry to disturb you but I'm looking for—"

Who the hell are you?

The voice climbed an octave, leaving the air quivering with its anger. So much for peace and goodwill, Gabe thought. Still, one caught more flies with honey. It was worth another try. "I'm looking for Caroline Donovan."

Go to hell.

"I don't think she lives there, but I suspect you do." Gabe couldn't resist the ungracious jab. There was no dealing with the old geezer. But he was the trespasser, he reminded himself, and took a firm hold on his patience. "If you could direct me—"

Gimme a beer.

That did it. Little ruffled Gabe, but standing in the peaceful countryside being verbally assaulted by the gruff demands of a Barbary Coast pirate annoyed him. He'd run afoul of a lunatic. He could only retrace his steps and find his error. He'd turned to go when he heard a sound as unexpected as it was welcome.

"Gabe!" Caroline's cry accompanied the crash of the door as it rebounded against its hinges. "You rang the bell."

"If that's an accusation, guilty as charged," he admitted, wondering why she scowled so fiercely at him. Then he looked at her and forgot to wonder. She wore gray corduroy jeans and a gray cotton sweater with a design of green and rose bands. Her hair was charmingly tousled and if her makeup was more than a pale lip gloss of raspberry sherbet, he couldn't detect it. Her feet were bare and impossibly small. And she was noticeably ill at ease.

"Nobody rings my doorbell," she said.

"Is there some law against it?"

Caroline tugged nervously at her sweater. The moment she'd anticipated with dread and longing had come. For days she'd thought of nothing but this man. Twice she'd sought out Julie Townsend. Julie, though not a gossip, had access to the information gleaned by the others who worked at the inn. Caroline learned then that Gabe's work was frequently clandestine and dangerous and more often than not in countries torn by war or unrest. His work was nonpolitical but no less perilous. The thought frightened her. She had tried desperately to put him from her mind, and had failed abysmally. Day after day she'd found herself searching for him at every corner, listening for his laugh.

When she had wakened in the night, her disturbing dreams filled with the seductive promise in his eyes, she'd named herself fool. Why should she risk involvement with a man who would leave her to wander the globe—a man who lived under the threat of death. She'd lost Mark and it had nearly destroyed her. She couldn't face that again. By actual count she'd only known Gabe for hours. No, not actually known— she'd been magnetized. From the moment he'd held her in his arms, laughing yet so worried for her, he'd dominated her thoughts. Time and again she'd remembered the richness of his dark hair and how it clung in stubborn waves at the nape of his neck. How blue his eyes had seemed, incandescent and burning in that strange, silent duel with Shiloh. For days she'd fought to forget the lazy elegance of his rugged strength and the toughness tempered by an easy gentleness he made no effort to conceal. But most unforgettable was that peculiar energy that seemed to burn between them. It was this that had destroyed her best efforts to sweep him from her mind.

Last night she had stood at her open window. Alone in the darkness, with the cotton lace of her gown cool like snow against her skin, the kiss of a night breeze on her face and only Gabe in her thoughts, she knew she must conquer this fascination. She must end the vulnerability that set her trembling at the mere thought of him. Forgetting the lateness of the hour, and reciting every fitting cliché she knew, she had dialed the inn. The instant she heard his voice—intimate, low and husky with sleep—she knew she'd made a mistake. And now he'd come, as handsome and compelling as she'd feared.

She struggled to draw herself from her thoughts and rushed to fill the expectant silence. "Of course there's no law against ringing the bell. I just thought you'd knock."

"I did, Caroline. Twice."

"Oh. I must have been in the bedroom looking for, uh, something." She was blankly flustered.

"Your shoes," Gabe suggested.

"Yes." Caroline looked down at her feet and her familiar grin burst through. "My shoes."

Gimme a beer.

Gabe flinched and tried to probe the shadows behind Caroline. "If something's come up, if there's a conflict, we can have dinner some other time."

"Don't be silly. Dinner's ready and waiting."

"In that case, I'd consider it a step in the right direction if you'd ask me in."

Shut up and kiss the broad.

"Shut up yourself, Joe," Caroline shouted into the shade of the foyer. Gabe watched as a flush rose to brighten her cheeks.

"I'd like to meet your friend," he said.

"My friend?"

"I believe you called him Joe."

"Joe!" Caroline clamped her hand over her mouth. Gabe thought it was in surprise, then he realized that it was laughter. She took her hand away once, started to speak, then lost herself in chuckles. "Joe! You think Joe will interrupt our dinner?"

"He does sound like an ornery codger."

"I'm sorry. I shouldn't laugh." She sputtered, then dissolved into helpless laughter.

Gabe folded his arms across his chest, torn by a natural inclination to join in the fun, but still puzzled.

Obscure and obscene, a perfectly accented dialect slashed through Caroline's laughter with a purring cackle. Gabe's arms dropped in surprise. His face paled at the advice he'd just been given. "Joe must be a character as well as a codger."

"He is that." She slipped her arm through his and led him into the heart of her home. He had little time to absorb its comfort as she dragged him to a corner where glass met glass and a profusion of plants and stones formed an oasis. Captured sunlight sparkled over water and dwelt naturally in the room. An artist had been given full rein with the design. More than an artist, a master of his craft who made the impossible easy and beauty simple.

From the foliage and between bars of gleaming brass a hooded gaze followed Gabe. At Gabe's silently indrawn breath Caroline stopped and waited expectantly. She watched as this lean, dark man looked implacably back into the wickedly bright gaze. She had seen steel and tenderness in him, and humor. Now she would gauge the scope of that humor. For reasons she refused to face, she hoped he wouldn't disappoint her.

The gazes battled forever. Then Gabe looked away, his eyes closed and his face impassive. A shudder passed through him. He lifted his gaze to Caroline's. "This, of course," he said, "is Joe."

"Yes."

"I've spent the last five minutes arguing with a scruffy, yellow-legged parrot?"

"I'm sorry, I didn't think you'd ring the bell," Caroline said.

"I don't think I've ever heard a parrot who sounds quite so human."

"I know. He's a rarity, and you're not the first person he's fooled."

A low rumble started deep in his chest, becoming a shout of laughter, resonant, full and unaffected. He laughed and it was wonderful.

"Stonebridge isn't quite the idyllic interlude it was meant to be," Gabe observed when his laughter dwindled into chuckles. "Chimney fires and pretty firemen and a runt called Joe. What next!"

Gimme a beer.

"That's next." Caroline was pleased by his response to the bird. "I'll get Joe his beer. Then we'll have peace."

When she'd gone Gabe spent a moment studying his nemesis. Joe was a stubby bird with a saffron head, green body and splashes of scarlet at his wings. Feet as yellow as his beak clung to a swaying perch. Preening most delicately, he dropped a translucent lid over one eye and then the other. A tilt of his heavy beak set the perch into a fast swing and his low mutter resembled a lullaby.

"Find the company boring do you?" Gabe asked. "I could say the same, but I won't. My mother taught me better manners. She was prettier too."

"Who was prettier?" Caroline had returned with a glass of golden liquid. At the cage she filled a small dish.

"My mother, is that really beer?"

"Of course not. Prettier than who?"

"Joe's mother."

"What's Joe's mother got to do with anything?" Caroline set the glass down and faced Gabe.

"Nothing."

"I see. I think."

"Of course you don't. Neither do I. That certainly looked like beer."

"Apple juice," Caroline backtracked as easily as he. This was the verbal badinage she relished. Gabe promised to be a formidable partner the likes of Shiloh and Mark before him. She could be comfortable: it would serve as a deterrent against the sensual undercurrent that swirled about them.

"Why apple juice?" Gabe asked, certain the answer would be as nonsensical as the bird himself.

"I can't give him beer, can I?"

"No, you certainly can't give him beer," Gabe agreed easily, then asked, "why can't you give him beer?"

"Because only apple juice makes him tipsy."

"Nobody gets tipsy on apple juice."

"This bird does."

Gabe groaned. "I should have known."

"Gabe, you need a drink."

"I know!"

"Scotch?"

"Thank God." He was relieved, he'd feared she'd offer apple juice.

Gabe's pleasure in Caroline's home increased when she led him to the dining alcove tucked into a corner of the large room. A small table was set for two, with wildflowers in the center. On an antique sideboard were chafing dishes filled with food.

"My compliments to the chef."

"Thank you." Caroline poured a white wine into two long-stemmed glasses, handed one to Gabe, then filled her plate and joined him at the table. They ate quietly with the haunting strains of a Spanish guitar tape Caroline had chosen in the background. Even the indistinct mutterings from Joe were of little consequence.

Pass the salt.

Absently Gabe picked up the shaker at his elbow, then stopped in midmotion. "You don't want the salt, do you?"

"No." Her smile widened at his wise deduction.

"Naturally." He set the shaker down with telling care, ignoring the culprit whose corner was now as silent as a tomb. The music had changed from haunting to seductive by the time Gabe laid down his fork and sighed.

"Dessert?" Caroline asked over the flickering candlelight. The play of its dancing shadows created hollows beneath her cheekbones highlighting the almond shape of her eyes. She was sophisticated and alluring;

the gamin of another day was a barefoot femme fa-
tale. He wondered which she would be when he made
love to her? And he would make love to her. He must.
The challenge of discovery, of catching her quicksil-
ver moods, haunted him night and day. The thought
of her lovely body accepting his caresses brought a
smile to his lips.

"Is that smile for dessert?"

"For a memory," Gabe murmured. "A memory yet
to be."

Caroline tried to read beyond his bland expression
and failed. "I don't think I understand. I don't think
I'll try."

"It's early yet, but you'll understand," Gabe said
cryptically, the training of a lifetime containing the
desire that had become his constant companion. "And
I promise you a memory."

Before he had promised her laughter and kisses.
And now memories. Could she be more than a name
and a face and a warm body? Or would she be a
pleasant interlude, its memory fading as life faded?
Caroline shivered.

"I have my memories." With four quiet words she'd
managed, at least for a moment, to shut him out. He'd
strayed into painful and forbidden territory. She had
Pete, she had memories of her own and she was complete. She needed no more. Especially not from this
vibrant man whose flashing smile was dangerous to
her well-ordered life. Pushing back her chair she rose,
taking his plate and her own. "I'll get dessert."

"Let it wait." Gabe's fingers circled her wrist, exerting no pressure, but his touch was enough to halt
her.

She looked down at the lean hand and remembered another hand that had touched her, so confident and young. A smile, bittersweet and melancholy, crossed her face, then was hidden by a teasing expression. "Wait? Who can wait for one of my desserts?"

Gabe saw the ragged edge of her smile and chose to play her game. For the moment he would let her take refuge in her armor of laughter. "After this meal I'll need to watch my weight for a week."

Caroline looked at his narrow thighs molded by hip-clinging khaki, and his lean waist. Her searching eyes roved over his broad chest and wide shoulders, over tanned features, handsome in a battered, irregular fashion, and came to rest at his mouth. His strong, white teeth gleamed from between smiling lips. Finally she met his gaze. "I doubt you ever need to watch your weight," she said, "but how about Irish coffee instead?"

"Perfect."

"It will only take a minute."

Gabe released her and she hurried away. He stood, tossed his napkin aside and strolled to the bookcases that reached from ceiling to floor. Trailing his hand over the backs of the heavy volumes, he read their titles. He hadn't been mistaken: Caroline's library was one the finest architect would envy. He took a book down and leafed through it. A name was scrawled on the title page. As Caroline entered, tray in hand, he read the bold signature, "Cameron Prescott Douglas."

She put the tray down and sat to pour steaming, dark liquid into fragile cups. She finished filling each from a whiskey decanter, then leaned back. "Cameron Douglas was my father."

Gabe replaced the book and joined her on the sofa. Caroline's father had been one of the foremost architects in the country. It explained this jewel of a home hidden away in the middle of nowhere. It gave new significance to the Douglas Construction Company on the outskirts of Stonebridge. "I've admired your father's work for years."

"He loved to design. When his sight failed, out of economic necessity he had to concentrate on local construction, but he still dreamed of buildings he'd never see."

"His last, the Corbett Building, was his best. Had his sight begun to fail then?"

Caroline's cup rattled violently in its saucer and she set it down hurriedly. "He'd accepted the inevitable. He knew it was to be his last project. Driving himself on it hurried his death. He never knew it won the award." She pronounced the name of the most coveted prize in architecture and steadied her hands by linking them in her lap. Her face was expressionless, shuttered.

Another taboo subject. Gabe wondered why. Carefully he took her clasped hands in his. Unlacing her fingers, he lifted one hand to his cheek, touching the base of a healing finger with his lips. "The men in your life have been interesting and exciting. Is there room for one more? Maybe not so interesting nor so exciting, but certainly willing."

Caroline sat quietly, not withdrawing her hand, not speaking. Gabe had always been adept at reading faces, but he had no idea what was in her mind. In the course of the evening she'd been delightful, warm, mischievous. With the glint of her irreverent humor lighting her eyes, she had been funny, unpredictable and unwittingly provocative. When he thought he understood her a bit, she slipped away like a will-o'-the-wisp. Where was she when her smile faded to bittersweet and her eyes darkened to the gray of a winter's sea? Why did she wear laughter like a shield?

Did his answer lie in the lost look on her face when she spoke of Mark, and the hint of sorrow that tinged her pride in Pete? Did the answer lie in unresolved grief and a regret long buried? He had to know, but he must go carefully. Probing without understanding could deepen old wounds. Gabe vowed again that he would never hurt Caroline. He would tear the beating heart from his body first. And what remained, Shiloh would cheerfully feed to the vultures.

"Trust me, Caroline. Please. I won't hurt you."

His voice was seductive, his persuasion gentle. It would be wonderful to be held, to be touched, to rest her head on a strong shoulder, to forget death and loss and loneliness. To feel loved again, just for a minute. It had been so long. Gracefully she swayed toward him, drawn to him, mesmerized by wanting. Oh Lord, she cried in her heart, so long. Her lips parted, her eyes had grown smoky before the sweep of her lashes hid them like a veil.

As Gabe took her into his arms he remembered the sweetness of their first embrace.

"Jeepers." The door banged shut in unison with the exclamation. "What're you sitting in the dark for, Mom?"

In a move as natural as if she had practiced it endlessly, Caroline left Gabe's arms and turned to the boy. "It isn't dark, Pete. And where are your manners?" she scolded. "Say hello to Mr. Jackson. Gabe, my son Peter Markham Donovan, the third."

"Aw, Mom." The boy half scowled, half grinned. "Can't you just say Pete?"

"Sorry," she chuckled. "Gabe, my son Pete."

Gabe stood and accepted the hand Pete furtively scrubbed on the seat of his pants. The boy was tall and thin. There was a strength in his grasp, but he moved awkwardly; growth had outstripped coordination. His skin was dark, his hair bleached a golden brown by the summer sun. Remembering a small, walnut-framed photograph on a desk near the bookshelves, Gabe suspected that when he reached maturity Pete, too, would be tall, heavily muscled, with hair and eyes of deep brown. He was a living memory and wholly his father's son.

"Good game?" Gabe nodded toward the tennis racket Pete had dropped by a can of balls and a sweatband.

"Nah. Got a rotten serve and I'm slow. That dumb Beth beat me again, Mom."

"Don't be a sore loser. Beth's a good friend."

"Not for long," Pete said darkly.

"Patience. You'll learn to handle the half foot you've grown this year." Caroline went to him, kissing his cheek. "Why don't you get a quick shower and read the book Shiloh sent."

"Okay. I'll say good-night to Joe first. Night, Mom. Nice to meet you Mr. Jackson. Maybe," he muttered as he shuffled to Joe's cage, "I should take up basketball."

"Don't forget your racket," Caroline reminded.

"I won't. Hey, Mom, Joe's sulking."

"I know, Gabe rang the doorbell."

"Oh, brother." Pete gathered up his tennis equipment and disappeared down the hall.

"Life's a little tough for him right now." She returned to the sofa and Gabe joined her.

"I suppose it is hard without a father." He touched the nape of her neck, one curl coiled about his finger.

"At least he had my dad for a while, and Shiloh's helped."

"He likes Shiloh?"

"Shiloh's the best thing since yellow tennis balls. If he said red was green, Pete wouldn't question. He'd just think that Shiloh knew something no one else did."

"I see," Gabe grimaced, decided he'd heard more than enough about this paragon, and changed the subject. "Caroline, what's with the bell and the bird?"

Caroline sighed and put from her mind the warm slide of his knuckles over her skin. "Considering your reception tonight I suppose you are curious. Joe hates any bell. They send him into a frenzy. You rang the bell three times; that got us his entire repertoire."

"Who taught him to swear?"

"He was most proficient when the original Peter Donovan got him out of South America nearly thirty years ago."

"He has quite a vocabulary."

"It rivals yours." She slanted a look at him.

"He does me one better. Have you any idea what he said?"

"Haven't the foggiest."

"It's just as well."

"Hey, don't look so stern. Joe only mimics sounds."

"I'm not so sure about this bird."

"Surely you're not angry!" Caroline said in surprise.

"I'm not angry. In fact I'm having the time of my life, or I was before."

"Before what?"

"Before we were interrupted. Now—" he moved a fraction closer "—where were we?"

Caught by another of his quick changes, she was unprepared. In a moment of daring and madness she answered the stirrings that had spread like ripples in a pond. "I think," she murmured, "you were about to kiss me."

"So I was." Exerting only a slight pressure, he drew her nearer. Her body was like silk against him and he groaned quietly.

Caroline's palms slid up the fabric of his shirt, her fingers resting lightly at the pulsing hollow of his throat. "So strong, so sure," she murmured. Her hands curved about his neck, her fingers tangling in his hair. As she looked gravely into his eyes Gabe wondered again what she was thinking. Here was the most expressive face he'd ever seen—direct, appealingly frank. Until the shutter fell like a wall. A wall no one was allowed to venture past. He'd already journeyed into uncharted waters, the next move was hers.

Caroline leaned toward him, her mouth lightly skimming his as if in experiment. Like a petal in the wind her kiss was delicate and fleeting. The heat of her mouth lingered on his even as she moved away. Her grave stare held his, deeper, darker, and as unfathomable as before.

Barely touching him she traced the rugged line of his jaw. At the corner of his lips she hesitated, then as her gaze fell like a kiss on them she whispered something soft and indistinguishable. Languorously her fingers threaded through his hair, cupping his head, drawing his mouth down to hers. Slowly, carefully, she kissed him, her mouth opening against his like a flower, her tongue like rough velvet against his in a caress that offered paradise. When at last she would have drawn away, his arms about her held her fast.

He waited, steeling himself for the laughter, the shield of bravado, wondering how he could face it. Instead she sighed, and the sound of it was as sweet as the kiss itself.

"Gabe." She called his name, only his name, as she leaned her head helplessly against his shoulder. Caught close in a hard embrace, she could feel the heat that rose from him like a force, enveloping, compelling, as exciting as it was frightening. "I didn't expect—" her voice was a shaky whisper "—I didn't know."

"Shh," He stopped her halting efforts. He had known. Somehow he had known from the first that she would be a flame in his arms that would burn them both. But as much as he wanted her it was too soon. When Caroline came to him, he wanted all questions answered, all fears laid to rest. "It's all right. As kisses go that was dynamite, and much as I hate to say it, I think it was enough for tonight."

Caroline knew the effort he made. He wanted her as desperately and as shockingly as she wanted him. His need was a living thing—in the hoarseness of his voice, the ragged beat of his heart, and in his body, hard and taut against her own. "We need safer ground—" she swallowed nervously "—maybe we should get down to business."

"Business?" Gabe's mind failed to grasp her meaning.

She slipped easily from his arms. Crossing to a desk she took a roll of white papers from a tube. Returning to the sofa she unrolled them. "These are the plans for remodeling the cabin your uncle left you."

"How do you happen to have these?"

"You contacted the Douglas Construction Company, didn't you?"

"I did. I build roads and dams, even airports, but not houses." He realized suddenly that in his distraction he'd missed the obvious. "You're Douglas Construction?"

"Since my father died I am," she said, "along with the best crew anyone could ask for."

"I see." Gabe's face was impassive, but his eyes were thoughtful.

"Here." Caroline flattened the curling papers, anchoring them with an ashtray and a figurine. "We've considered the surroundings. I think that you'll find our changes preserve the age of the house while making it more comfortable. If you want other changes I'll be glad to make them."

She'd became the ultimate businesswoman, a role she assumed as naturally as she did everything else. If Gabe had doubts, one glance at the plans were enough to resolve them. The small house, drawn in bold lines, had been modernized even as its antiquity had been preserved. It was a stunning piece of work. There was only the rustle of papers as he studied the drawings in awe.

Misunderstanding his silence, Caroline rushed to reassure him. "There will be no problem if you decide to go with another design. This is simply a suggestion."

"Who designed your house, Caroline?"

"I did."

"Who built it?"

"My crew and I."

"And whose designs are these?"

"Mine."

"Then we'll go with them." With a nod and a smile the deal was sealed. Then, totally absorbed in the plans, they lost track of time until the clock struck twelve and drew a startled squawk from Joe.

"It's midnight!" Caroline exclaimed. "Where did the time go?"

"Sorry. I didn't mean to stay so late, but we accomplished a lot. When will you start?"

"Getting the road into passable condition is our first priority. We'll take the dozers in first thing tomorrow. Unless there are problems with loose shale, we should be on the site no later than two weeks."

Disturbed by the clock, Joe began a raucous outcry that grated on ear and nerves. Gabe cast him an exasperated glare. "Don't you have a cover for that cage?"

"He hates that. He'll stop when the lights are out."

"Then walk me to the door. We wouldn't want him to strain his voice. Although on second thought..."

Caroline grinned and slipped her arm through his. At the door Gabe wanted to take her into his arms but he knew he dared not. He might not be strong enough to resist her a second time. Instead he took her hand in both of his and lifted it to his lips. "It was a delightful evening, even if you never found your shoes."

"Omigosh!" In astonishment she looked down at her feet. "I didn't!"

Gabe released her hand and tapped her lightly on her upturned nose. "Before I go, there's something I should tell you."

"There is?"

"Uh-hmm," he nodded. "You have very sexy toes."

"Good night, Gabe." Her laugh was happy and comfortable as she pushed him out the door.

"Good night, Caroline."

Good night, sweetheart, Joe added grumpily as the door closed.

Four

The sun was high when Gabe brought his car to a halt, his passage blocked by a tangle of vine and stone. From here the road was impassable. His uncle had despised the automobile, preferring a horse-drawn wagon. The rough track no doubt served him nicely, but Caroline and her crew would find it difficult turning it into a negotiable thoroughfare.

He'd intended to come earlier but a call from Sam Danton—a friendly chat that was in reality a verbal medical exam—delayed him. After convincing Sam he'd had only one headache and no vertigo in weeks, Gabe managed to escape. The delay left him uncommonly irritable, and the stifling heat on the stony road he walked did nothing to improve his temper.

He topped the last rise expecting to hear the drone of machines and was astonished by silence. Then he heard the laughter of men lounging beneath the trees.

Gravel scattered beneath his feet as he stalked toward them. "What in hell's going on here?" he asked in a controlled voice that emphasized his anger. "I'm not paying you to sit on your backsides. Who's in charge? Where's Caroline?"

A small, bald man got to his feet, drew himself up to the fullest of his height and cocked an unimpressed eye at Gabe. "Don't get your dander up, Mac. You'll get your day's work. A Douglas crew never cheated anyone yet. Answering your first question, I'm Scotty Smith, foreman, but Caroline's in charge. As for your second question—" he shifted slightly so he could see past Gabe "—she's right there. We hit loose dirt that might set up a slide. She's gone to check it. Soon as we know what she's decided, you'll get your day's work."

What Gabe saw made his heart nearly catapult from his chest, fear clutched at him with a frozen hand. An anguished moan tore from him as he began to run.

"Heaven help me." He had no idea that he breathed the prayer as he scaled a steep embankment. Scooping a startled Caroline into his arms he spun to race back down the slope. He was an agile man. He lost his footing only once as the pounding of his footsteps dislodged the precarious hold of granite and shale mixed with soil. The small slide triggered a larger one, and he was only half a step ahead as it barrelled down the hillside. A desperate leap took them to safety.

The slide ended quickly, leaving behind an eerie silence and a blinding fog of suffocating dust. The men who had watched helplessly from a distance waited, frozen in shock. One pale man started toward the pile of rubble; Scotty's hand at his arm and a shake of his head stopped him. "She's not hurt," Scotty said.

"But she'll be madder than hell. Leave them be, let them settle it between them."

As if some invisible force served them as fearful reminder, a stone at the top of the wall slid partway down, bounced against another, then landed in a clatter at Gabe's feet. He stared at it, shuddered, then looked into the blazing eyes of his burden. "Dammit!" he thundered. "You did it again."

"I did it!"

"Yes. You!"

"Put me down, Gabe," Caroline said icily. "Then perhaps you'd be so kind as to explain what I've done. *Then* you can tell me what the devil you mean by interfering."

Gabe set her feet on the uneven terrain, his hands curled about her waist. He knew she was unharmed, but still shaken by what might have been, the contact reassured him. As he glared at her, his grudging approval of what he saw did little to mollify his frightened anger. She was dressed appropriately in jeans, a light blue denim shirt and boots. Except for a stray curl or two, none of her hair was visible beneath a yellow hard hat. She was so beautiful it hurt. Too beautiful to lose. All he'd felt in the past moments erupted in worried indignation. "Do you have a suicide complex? Any fool could see that bank was unstable and likely to let go at any minute. If a stone hadn't killed you, you'd have died of suffocation before we could dig you out. First the roof of the inn, now this. Dammit!" His fingers tightened convulsively, possessively. "You need a keeper."

"Let me go, Gabe," Caroline said, her tone a warning.

"Not until you explain."

"You've contracted for a job, not explanations."

Before he could reply she pushed against him with strength fueled by disgust. As she twisted away, his flailing hand glided over her breast and its delicate crest. But as she stepped away Gabe needed no tantalizing reminders that she was all woman.

She stood, feet planted firmly apart, fists clenched at her hips, her injured palm ignored but protected by its bandage. Her chin rose to a fighting angle. In the bright light of the sun, with red dust clinging to her face and clothing, and her cheeks flushed, she was magnificently furious. Through narrowed eyes she stared at him coldly, her rage beyond heated words.

"Don't ever do that again, Gabe." She spoke conversationally but the flash of her eyes left little doubt that she meant it.

"That wall of shale is dangerous," he insisted.

"Yes, it is and I know it. It's my job to know. This isn't the first time I've checked a dangerous site; I can assure you it won't be the last. Oddly enough, I've managed to survive this long without your help, and when you're gone, I suspect I'll continue. Granted, you were there at the inn when I did need you, and I'm grateful, but you've overstepped yourself today.

"You commissioned us to do this work, and we will—without interference—or we won't do it at all. This was interference as well as stupidity." She paused, drew a breath and shook her head in exasperation. "Have you stopped even one minute to consider why *I* was there rather than one of the men?"

"I don't suppose I was thinking," Gabe admitted.

"Suppose you start now," Caroline drawled. "You're an intelligent man, it shouldn't be too difficult for you."

"The slope is unstable."

"I think we've established that." There was no relenting in her posture.

"It's logical that the lightest and fastest person would check it out."

Her answer was a curt nod.

"Without inspecting your crew, I'd hazard a guess that would be you."

"Cute." She refused to be placated.

Gabe sighed heavily and looked away. For a painful second his attention was centered on the ravaged embankment. "I've been an idiot."

"I won't argue the point."

"My added weight and the shock of my footsteps caused a slide that could have killed us both."

"We were lucky."

"Point taken. I won't interfere again."

"Good."

"I would've fired any member of a crew who did what I just did," Gabe admitted.

"So would I." Caroline turned away.

"Wait," he called. "Where are you going?"

"Do you see that?" She jerked a thumb toward a bulldozer with a track as tall as she.

"I'd have to be blind not to."

"Just checking." Caroline almost smiled. "To answer your question, I'm going to get on that piece of machinery, and I'm going to cut down that bank."

Gabe was familiar with the equipment. He knew better than most that operating it required skill and strength. "Caroline," he protested in spite of his promise not to interfere. "You can't!"

"I can't?"

"No. You can't," he repeated doggedly.

"How very fortunate for me that you're here, Gabe." She smiled sweetly at him, a smile that had as much warmth as a glacier. "I've been doing this for over fifteen years, and nobody ever bothered to tell me I couldn't." She turned away, dismissing this conversation and the man.

"Nobody? Not even your precious Shiloh? He certainly hovers enough." Gabe regretted the words instantly.

Caroline stopped, not believing her ears. For an instant she didn't move, then she whirled to face him. "No," she said too quietly, after a silence that seemed endless, "not Shiloh. Especially not Shiloh."

For the first time in years Gabe felt a blush burn his neck and cheeks. There was no more he could say as he watched her stalk to the great machine, climb aboard, engage the engine, and move it toward the slide.

"Caroline has a wicked temper." The crew chief had come to stand by Gabe's side, his voice a gruff shout over the tractor's roar.

"So I found out."

An engine coughed, sputtered. The monstrous bulldozer lurched. Shale slid beneath its track and Caroline backed it slowly away.

"Ah, God." Gabe barely breathed.

"I know," Scotty sympathized. "She shouldn't do it, yet she does. If it's any consolation, she's one of the best."

"Forgive me," Gabe said through tightly clenched teeth. "That doesn't help."

"No, it doesn't, does it?" Scotty patted him on the shoulder and moved toward the men gathered by the tree. Every eye was fixed on Caroline.

"All right," Scotty shouted, "show's over. Mr. Jackson here wants a day's work for a day's pay."

The men scattered over the roadbed, the incident put from their immediate thoughts but not forgotten. Gabe saw familiar faces among the crew. A few days ago many of them had worn the gear of volunteer firemen. This crew proved to be as good at working together. They were a unit and the hub was Caroline.

Soon, growing restless as a spectator, Gabe shucked his shirt and joined in sorting unearthed stones for a retaining wall. The work was hard and dirty, but did little to numb his nagging worry for Caroline's safety. Intent on waging mental and physical war on his anxiety, he was startled by a shrill whistle.

"Break for lunch," Scotty called, then waved to Caroline.

With a grin, she cut the engine, slid off her hat and climbed down. As she walked among her men who sat in clusters in the shade, there were invitations to share lunch with them. "No, thanks," she declined. "I'm heading to the creek to wash away some dirt."

From a cooler in the truck's cab she took a brown bag and a soft drink. Gabe watched as she moved away from the group. He wiped his hands and face with a bandana Scotty had given him, slipped on his shirt and followed.

There were invitations for Gabe, too. The men were leery of this newcomer at first. Then when it was clear that he could work with the best of them, he'd been accepted without reservation. With an appreciative wave he refused. "Think I'll stroll down and join Caroline."

As he crossed the meadow, the swift rush of the stream muted a murmur of voices. Caroline was not alone.

"It's a wee bit hard ye were on him, lass." Scotty lapsed, as he often did, into the soft brogue of his native Scotland. "Ye must remember what a shock 'twould be for a man who's niver seen the likes. Do ye ken my own reaction. Nearly gave me a heart attack, ye did, first time ever your dad let you crawl up on one of the big monsters."

Caroline murmured something that Gabe couldn't hear, it was lost and swept away by the splash of the creek.

"I know, lass. But ye must be patient. He'll learn."

Underbrush snagged Gabe's hair and caught at his clothing. His foot slipped against a deadfall. It cracked like a rifle, but neither Scotty nor Caroline heard.

"He's a man of the world, an engineer who knows the land, but he has more to learn than he knows. You're a woman beyond his ken and . . . Ach." Scotty shrugged and patted her cheek in a loving gesture. "I'm a meddling old fool. Have your lunch and pay me no mind." Grumbling as he went, the little man took the direct path Gabe had missed.

A vine tangled about Gabe's ankle, he bent to strip it away. When he was free Scotty was out of sight and Caroline was slipping the tail of her already unbuttoned shirt from the waist of her pants. He pushed aside the shrub ready to step into the clearing when one flick at each wrist and a shrug of her shoulders sent the shirt into a heap on the grass. Gabe knew he should call out, that he should warn her of his presence, but his tongue lay useless in his dry mouth.

He was mute as she dropped to her knees by the stream, her hands cupped to splash water over her face and neck. As she wiped drops of moisture from her eyes he could see that the white cotton camisole she wore was transparent in its dampness. It clung like skin to her firm breasts. Beneath their veil of white her nipples were darkening shadows as they contracted with the chill. Her midriff tapered to a waist that was astonishingly slender. In contrast, the globes of her breasts appeared fuller, an invitation to a lover's caress.

Gabe stifled a raw groan in its silence and his body grew taut in his tenuous control.

Twice more as he watched, unable and unwilling to break the enchantment, she repeated the ritual. In concession to her strenuous morning, she rested her hands at her neck, flexed her shoulders and kneaded the tired muscles. Then with her arms extended she arched her back and offered her face to the drying heat of the sun. She was a golden flame inviting him into the inferno. Her image burned indelibly in his heart, and he knew she was more than a challenge, more than a balm for his sexual needs.

He watched unashamedly as she rose, plucked her shirt from the grass and slipped it on. The impulse to call out to her, to stay the hand that closed the buttons, was strong. He resented that any part of her was hidden from him. He wanted all of her—here, now, in the sunlight. But Caroline wasn't ready for what he felt. He would bide his time. He would learn to be a man of patience.

When she was dressed, her shirt neatly tucked into her waistband, he deliberately stepped on a limb. It cracked as loudly as before, this time Caroline heard. "Scotty?"

"No, Gabe." He stepped into the clearing, pretending nonchalance as she waited for him to join her. He was the first to speak. "I'm sorry."

There was no reply from Caroline.

He shifted uncomfortably. In a concerted effort he put her sunlit image from his mind. Apologies weren't his style, they didn't come easily. "I made a fool of myself and I'm asking you to forgive me."

There was an almost imperceptible relaxing of her rigid stance but Caroline remained silent.

"Blast it!" Gabe's temper got the best of him. "How the hell was I to know you were some sort of expert with the damnable equipment?"

She continued to look at him. He knew she waited for something more.

"I've apologized. What more do you want?" He ran a hand through his sweat-flattened hair. He was accustomed to being the one who made his quarry squirm, but he could take lessons from Caroline. He knew what she expected. With a heavy sigh he complied. "I shouldn't have said what I did about Shiloh. It was...unnecessary." Gabe couldn't bring himself to admit the pettiness of jealousy.

"Yes, it was. Shiloh's a friend. A good one. He wouldn't dream of meddling in my work." Her low voice carried over the intruding sounds.

"Apology accepted?" Gabe asked hopefully.

"Accepted," she conceded. "Now, how about some lunch? I have an extra sandwich."

"I thought you'd never ask." He grinned in relief. "What have you got? I'm starved."

"My favorite. Peanut butter and jelly."

"I should have known," he groaned.

"For proletarian tastes there's roast beef." Her smile was wicked as she offered a roll with thick slices of beef spilling out.

The day set a pattern. Caroline was delighted as the crew assumed an easy friendship with Gabe as he lent a hand wherever it was needed. He was no longer "Mr. Jackson," but "Gabe" and sometimes "Hey you." A week aged into two and it became commonplace to see him by her side. His dark head was always bent low toward hers, his attention totally at her command, as he matched his stride with hers.

Gabe never again made the mistake of reacting to the improbable things she did. If she chose to drive a heavily loaded truck across a narrow ledge, for all that he cringed inside he never voiced his fear. She took a certain satisfaction in teasing him with a look or a gesture that asked, aren't you going to remind me that I can't do this? His response was always a shake of his head, a shrug, and a grin that meant, I wouldn't dare.

He was thankful that she never knew how often his heart was in his throat, nor how frequently his hands were clenched against the need to snatch her from some danger. Gradually he began to understand that she was never foolhardy or careless, never undertook a task she couldn't meet. In that he found some small comfort. She did delegate to the stronger and the fittest. Caroline had nothing to prove; she was a woman who had a job to do and she did it to the best of her abilities. She judged a man on his merits and looked for the same in herself.

Gabe knew the crew accepted their relationship at face value. Only Scotty, with his wry grins, saw beneath the surface. It was he who remarked sotto voce how often Gabe sought her out, and how often she laughed while looking into his eyes. It was Scotty who voiced to Gabe his secret pleasure that Caroline opened to him like a flower to the sun.

Gabe discovered Scotty was a mine of information. As they worked together he learned the bits and pieces that made the whole. Scotty's loyalty had always lain with the Douglas family and was strongest to Caroline. He'd been with her through the joys of triumph and the loneliness of tragedy. While Shiloh came offering condolence and comfort after Mark's death, Scotty had hoped she'd found more than a friend, then was silent in his disappointment.

"Maybe this time," the little man said as much to himself as to Gabe. "Caroline won't admit it, but she needs someone who'll be more than a friend, someone who can help her forget she's the widow Donovan."

"Shiloh's been away on a business trip for a week, I seem to have stepped into his shoes as special friend and companion," Gabe said grimly. "It's a barrier I can't get past."

"Oh, I'm not so sure." A smile touched Scotty's razor-thin lips. "I think that more than once this week, you've made our tomboy remember she's really the lovely Caroline."

"I hope you're right," Gabe said honestly. He had long ago ceased to hide what he felt for Caroline from this wily man. "I keep telling myself to be patient, that she's worth waiting for."

"Your intentions are honorable then, are they?"

"I can't say that I'm ready for home and hearth, but I won't harm her, if that's what you mean."

"'Tis enough. 'Honorable' is a bit different than it was in my day—" Scotty chuckled "—the dark ages, you know. I won't tell you what to do. I doubt you'd listen any more than the lass. Just be patient."

"I'm trying, Scotty."

But as Caroline continued to keep him at arm's length in her warm, friendly way, Gabe discovered patience was harder than he thought. He grew increasingly somber and leaner as he turned more and more to the work that had become the outlet of his pent-up frustrations.

In the heat of a late-August day at the end of the second week, Caroline watched as Gabe picked up a heavy sledge-hammer and a long steel spike. He walked to the retaining wall, his hair falling over the bandana tied about his forehead and sweat gilding his skin. Muscles rippled and knotted, the hammer swung in an arc, driving the spike into the packed earth. It was the last; the road was finished.

As she climbed from her now silent machine, Caroline was remembering that those powerful arms had held her. They had been gentle. She wondered if they would be again. She'd tried to forget the feel of his arms about her and his lips on hers. Here among the men, working and laughing with him, she'd drawn a veil of illusion about their growing friendship, pretending it was nothing more. But in the solitude of the night, when her secret thoughts ran free, she knew he had become more than a friend.

At the signal from Scotty the men gathered about her on the smooth roadbed. She dismissed them and wished them a good weekend. As they scattered she turned to Gabe, waiting while he put his tools away.

"It's a good road," she said as he finished his task, closing and locking the temporary toolshed.

"Yes, it is," he agreed and lapsed into silence.

"A job well done deserves a celebration."

"What did you have in mind?"

"A picnic?" Caroline heard the tentativeness in her voice. In the past few days the easy laughter had suddenly become rare. Gabe had worked like a demon, a grim expression on his face, and at times he'd seemed withdrawn. As he grew darker and more brooding, the current that flowed between them grew stronger. It now rose like heat in Caroline and she almost backed away. "I thought we might..." she stammered, swallowed, and tried a smile that wouldn't come. "It was just a foolish idea."

"Shall we go down by the creek?" Gabe asked as if he hadn't heard her faltering.

"Yes," Caroline murmured. "I'd like that." Their gazes held. In them was the knowledge that today would be different from the days they'd shared lunch in the shade of an oak.

From the cab of the truck she brought a hamper heavy with food, wine and linen. No brown bags and peanut butter for this day. Gabe took the basket and silently walked with her over the meadow.

A breeze played among the oak leaves, their rustle crisp with the first hint of brown. The grass where Caroline and Gabe had sat in dusty jeans and boots seemed lusher, a carpet for the blanket she spread over it.

Gabe had never forgotten the day he'd watched Caroline wash at the water's edge. He'd begun to wash there himself after their lunch each day.

Today a few droplets of mountain-cooled water wouldn't be enough. He needed more to temper his passion. He needed the bite of a deep, frigid pool—a shock to clear his head, to keep him from snatching her into his arms and loving her, hard and quickly, with all the fire that burned within him.

Caroline had been hardly past childhood when Mark had been taken from her, and through the years she'd known no lover. The barriers of her youthful love had left her innocent. No temptations lurked in the limbo of the faithful where she'd abode for ten years. She'd come through the morass of grief and the years of widowhood a woman of strength, but no less untried in the ardor of an adult than the young Caroline. Strong in so many ways and yet fragile, she might be frightened by the inflaming torment of maturity. It was there, that sleeping passion, and to awaken it slowly, Gabe knew he must cool his own. A misstep now could be disastrous.

"I think I'll go downstream for a quick swim to wash away the dust." He hardly recognized his own voice. "I'll be back for the celebration before you know it."

Caroline looked up and nodded her understanding. Intent on getting away while he still could, Gabe he was not aware that her gaze followed him until the underbrush blocked him from sight.

With her hands clasped, her head bent over the blurred reflection in the moving water, Caroline was still, pensive, and a little afraid. The quiet surrounded her and the world seemed to wait. Her fears of loving and losing retreated to the distant recesses of her mind. At least for this small moment, they seemed not to matter. She shivered gently and sighed, accepting the inevitable. Then, rousing herself, with a secret smile she began to open the buttons of her shirt.

As Gabe stepped into the clearing he had eyes only for Caroline. She lay beneath the oak, with her head pillowed by an arm. She wore her jeans and as always a camisole of snowy cotton. Her boots were gone, the belt to her jeans tucked in one, her damp shirt hung from a stunted cherry tree. Her breathing was slow and easy, pressing her breasts into the folds of fabric gathered to a band of tatted lace. Droplets of water clung to her, gleaming like pearls against her skin. Her lashes lay like fans at her cheeks, her lips were curved in a half smile, her cheeks were dewy and flushed. A half-finished glass of wine tipped precariously in her hand.

Gabe wondered if she slept. He moved closer, carefully gliding through the last clump of brambles. A rivulet of water trickled over his bare chest and he absently dried it with his shirt. He made no sound but she sensed he was there. Her eyes fluttered open dreamily.

"Gabe." Her voice was low and sweet, a little breathless as if she were surprised to see him standing over her. She wasn't. She'd been waiting for his footstep. And after a lifetime he was here, staring down at her.

"Are you hungry?" Her voice was unsteady and her heart thudded. She found she truly was breathless.

"Only for you," he said thickly as if the words were dragged from him against his will. Every promise of care and caution escaped him, gone as if never made. His heart ruled his head and he only knew he wanted her.

His words echoed through her, the haunting melody of an unwritten song. "Yes," she whispered, her arms lifting, opening, eager for him. "Yes, Gabe. Yes."

He was on his knees. He didn't know if they buckled beneath him or if he knelt. It didn't matter. Nothing mattered except the feel of Caroline's arms about him, the touch of her lips on his. His chest was pressed against her breasts. The lacy camisole was but a gossamer film, yet even it was too much. He wanted nothing between them, he wanted her skin like silk against his. He tugged at the barrier, then the delicate cotton was gone and with it her jeans. And then his own.

Her breath was short, ragged; he could almost feel her heart beating as he touched her. Far-flung promises tugged at him—dimly, fading, but enough to draw him from her. As the warmth of his body left hers, she trembled.

"Darling." Her hand curved about his shoulder, drawing him back to her. "Don't be afraid," she whispered. "I won't hold you or try to keep you. There's no tomorrow, there's only today. Now. This minute."

Then his lips were on hers, kissing her, caressing her. His tongue touched hers and waves of pleasure swept through them, one to the other, a scintillating flame. She was warm, she was luscious. There was a fierceness in her that allowed him no restraint, no holding back. When her body began an unconscious undulation against his, straining closer and closer, almost wild in her need for him, he slid over her, joining their bodies, fusing them in a move that was as gentle as it was urgent. They were belly to belly, breast to breast, yet he cradled her from the crush of his weight. Their mouths joined. She met his power with a velvet strength.

In a dream come true he felt her response, no more than the flutter of a butterfly, embracing him in the ecstasy of love. She cried his name, holding him in her shattering caress, and he quaked in fulfillment.

As the rustling leaves cast lacy shadows over them, he gathered her to him, her flushed skin hot when she nestled languidly against his shoulder. He stared at the horizon, his mind filled with wonder. For all her innocence, Caroline had shown him gratification as he'd never known it. He had been the innocent in passion and she his mentor. What magic did she possess? What had she given him that no woman ever had?

His mind whirled with questions as he stroked her hair and murmured drowsily, "Sleep, love. Sleep."

Gabe woke. His arms were empty, the blanket had been drawn over him. Caroline stood by the creek, dressed in camisole and jeans, struggling with the button at her waist. Once, twice, it slipped from her shaking fingers.

"Are you all right?" he asked quietly.

"I'm fine." She didn't look at him as she at last succeeded with the button.

"We never had our picnic."

"No."

He waited, hoping she would say more, or that she would at least look at him. Instead she bent to pull her boots on, hurriedly and as clumsily as she'd been with her jeans.

"Caroline. Look at me."

Her shoulders tensed, he could almost see the muscles there knot. Her head lifted, her eyes, blank and unreadable, met his. Still she didn't speak.

"Have dinner with me. Stay with me." His voice was hoarse with strain. "We'll only talk, if that's what you want, but come home with me."

"I can't." She shook her head and looked away. "I can't. Shiloh's back and I promised Pete... I'm sorry, Gabe."

Before he realized what she intended, she snatched her shirt from the tree and was striding across the meadow. He watched her until she was hidden from view, knowing it was futile to try to stop her. He lay there long after the rumble of her truck faded in the distance. His gaze traveled over his corner of the meadow, over the undisturbed picnic basket, the spilled goblet, the crushed grass where Caroline had lain.

For a while this had been their world, a secret glade, with only the sky and the earth to contain them. She'd been open and giving, more wonderful than he would have believed. Then the wall had come down, shutting him out.

"Why, Caroline? Why are you suddenly so afraid?" His question seemed to echo endlessly over the empty meadow.

Five

Gabe stepped through the archway to the dining room. As always, the room was dimly lit and soft music flowed from a hidden stereo. Several candlelit tables were occupied and from them rose a low hum of conversation. Julie Townsend moved about the room chatting, offering fresh coffee, tea, or the occasional cocktail. Tall and dark, with her hair pulled back in a sleek chignon, she was stately rather than awkward in her last stages of pregnancy.

Gabe waited while she replenished the cup before Shiloh Butler. Light flickered over Shiloh's face, the livid scar that rent his face darkening in the faint glow. He was intimidating, sitting alone at his secluded table. But not to Julie; she addressed him with the ease of an old friend. "How does Caroline seem tonight?"

"Happy, proud, and in spite of herself a little blue, a little edgy. But she tries to hide that part of it," Shiloh answered.

"I'm glad you finished your business early."

"So am I, but I would have been here at any rate."

"You're always here when she has something to face."

"There's not a lot I can do to help."

"Don't kid yourself." Julie patted his shoulder. "Just having you here helps."

"I'd like to think that's true."

"Take it from another woman, it helps not to be all alone." She touched his shoulder one more time and smiled. "Now, if you'll excuse me, I'd better attend to my duties before the management fires me."

Julie hurried toward Gabe, a friendly greeting on her lips. She was an instinctive and gracious hostess. Shiloh and the Stonebridge Inn were fortunate in her, Gabe thought.

"How's Mom today?" he asked as she drew near.

"Expanding and blooming," she answered cheerfully. "A table and a menu?"

"A table. No menu. Coffee, please."

"No sooner said than done." Julie led him to a table by the window overlooking the creek. When he was seated she filled his cup and asked, "Can't I get you something else?"

"No, thanks. But some company would be nice. Do you think Butler would mind if you joined me for one cup?"

Julie looked at her watch. "I'm due a break. Let me make one more round and I'll be back."

Gabe sipped the steaming liquid gingerly, watching Julie circle the room, his eyes straying often to the solitary Shiloh. Two cups sat on the table but there was no other indication Caroline had been there.

"If the invitation still holds—" Julie had returned "—I'll join you. No coffee for me these days, but I'd love to just sit."

"Tough day?"

"Only because Junior decided this was the day he'd practice tap dancing up and down my spine." She eased her bulk into the chair that Gabe held for her, sighing in relief.

Noting the look of bliss that crossed her face he chuckled. "When's Junior due?"

"With my luck, in the middle of the Harvest Ball."

"That's October, isn't it?"

"Right. The high point of the Autumn Festival, when Stonebridge steps back in time and becomes an early Colonial village. As tired as I am of hauling this baggage," she patted her stomach lovingly, "I'd hate to miss the fun."

"You're an unusual woman," Gabe commented.

"Pregnancy, even at my age, is a fact of life. Why hide myself away because my shape's not what it used to be?" Gabe looked again at Shiloh's table and Julie realized his attention had drifted away. "Looking for Caroline?"

"I thought she might be here," he admitted.

"She was. She is. She's checking on Pete. He and his friends are having a party down at the picnic grounds. No adults allowed."

"A special occasion?"

"You might call it that. Tomorrow's the first day of the fall session at the Stonebridge Academy and Pete's first year there."

"He'll live on campus?" Gabe hadn't known; Caroline never talked about what hurt. It was a part of herself she never shared.

"A requirement." Julie made a soft sound of sympathy. "She's going to miss that kid. They've been so close, it will be hell letting go."

"That's why Butler's back." It wasn't a question but a foregone conclusion.

"He knew Pete's leaving would be hard on Caroline and he likes to be here for her when he can."

"So I've noticed." A wry smile twisted Gabe's lips. His gaze met Shiloh's as Julie rattled on.

"Maybe all of us can keep her from being so lonely until she gets used to the idea. I hope so, anyway." Julie pushed back her chair and rose. "It's time I got back to work."

Unnoticed, Caroline watched from the darkness. She'd known this moment had to come, but she'd hoped for time to think. How could she answer the question Gabe had the right to ask? She had deliberately enticed him to make love to her, had offered herself without reservation, then run away like a child. How could she explain the seething chaos of her thoughts in the aftermath—the keen cut of guilt, the wonder of loving, the fear of losing?

This afternoon she'd gathered her tattered pride and her confusion about her and galloped like a frightened colt across the meadow. But she'd discovered one couldn't run from memories. She would carry them with her forever, like a painting in her mind. Memories of the whispering music of the brook, the glint of sunlight in his hair, the fragrance of grass crushed beneath their bodies, his hand, hard and callused and so very gentle, holding her, loving her, would be with her always.

In the hours since, as she'd profoundly searched the depths of soul and self, she'd finally admitted some hard-won truths and laid to rest her guilt. The genesis of all her truths was that today there had been no betrayal. Mark, a selfless, loving man, would have been the last to ask that she live unfulfilled. Her mind and her body had known. Only her heart hadn't relinquished the last precious link. Until Gabe.

Gabe! His name was a cry of pleasure and of torment.

Beneath the sting of a frigid shower she had washed the haunting scent of him from her body, stripping away the languor of a pleasure like none she'd ever known. Then, swathed in a terry robe, she'd wandered aching and lonely in her own home. Finally, huddled in a corner of a terrace that overlooked a meadow, she faced the source of her torment.

Gabe could be no more than an interlude. Sweet, passionate, beautiful, but an interlude. He would be healed soon and would move on. It was best. He was a man with a wanderlust, a stranger to all she held most precious. Even with his plans for the cabin, he had no roots, needed no home. He'd come to Stonebridge hurt and vulnerable, but the lure of the world would soon call to him and, no matter what was between them, he must answer. She'd already borne the loneliness of waiting for the man she loved, and survived the desolation of his loss. She couldn't again.

This, not the enchantment of the attraction they shared, was the flesh and blood of reality. The differences in their lives were shattering and irreconcilable. She must accept and remember until the time when he would leave her. But until that day she must deny her need for him. But could she? This afternoon she had run away and discovered that, like memories, she couldn't run from what had become part of her.

A frisson of uncertainty gripped her as she hesitated in the shadows, but she fought it. She would do what she must. She would smile and laugh and face this as she had a thousand things before. For the moment she would concentrate on Pete, and on tomorrow with all its joy and sadness.

She would take one problem at a time. Squaring her shoulders, pasting a smile on her face, she stepped into the light. She was a mother returned from soothing her parental anxiety; her expression was serene. "Hi, Julie, Gabe."

"Caroline," he murmured her name. It was a caress, not a greeting. He had to fold his fingers into his palms to steady them. He wanted to touch her. But he dared not. Beneath the smooth arch of her brow her eyes were glazed with troubled thoughts, and behind the facade of the brave smile trembling on her lips, she'd locked herself away from him. He was helpless in his need to comfort her.

"How were the boys?" he asked casually, hoping to calm the invisible turbulence that pulsated in her.

"What?" She started, her hand going to her throat, the fixed smile withering on her lips.

"I asked you about Pete," he said as gently as he could. She was like a butterfly, poised to flee at the first sign of threat. Her face was pale, her cheeks flushed and her eyes enormous. In her gauzy dress, with its creamy lace framing her throat, she was lovely. Caroline always wore lace, delicate, hidden, touching her skin as he would. Even now a sprig of Queen

Anne's lace was tucked behind her ear, its clusters of tiny flowers brushing the satin of her cheek. In the dancing candlelight she looked young, innocent. It seemed impossible she was the mother of a son; impossible that she'd lain like a lover in his arms with only sunlight for her clothing and leafy shadows for her lace.

The old familiar stirrings began in him, as urgent and keen as if the moment were now.

"How about the hot-dog-eating contest?" Julie asked, oblivious to the malaise that spun like a tangled web between them.

"It should be beginning about now." Caroline looked away from Gabe, glad of the release Julie offered.

"My money's on Pete." Julie was definite.

"Mine too," Gabe added.

"Mine too, I'm afraid." Caroline moaned. "Tonight, instead of packing his footlocker, he could be unpacking his stomach."

"Ha!" Julie disagreed. "Have you forgotten? Kids have cast-iron stomachs. Oh-oh," she muttered before Caroline could reply, "a customer. See you later."

"Julie's right, you know," Gabe said when they were alone. "He'll survive. Don't tell me the daredevil of roofs and earth movers never did anything crazy."

Relief made Caroline's knees weak. He didn't mean to press her, he wasn't angry. "Actually, I did." Her sudden laugh was deep, hearty and natural. "I could eat more peanut-butter-covered marshmallows than anyone in the seventh grade."

"And you survived. So will Pete."

"I'm convinced. I suppose he'd consider winning to be worth the price. He was in training all day. He only ate three eggs and a bowl of grits for breakfast, then for an evening snack he ate sparingly—an entire pizza and half a chocolate pie. A fast, so he would be properly hollow for the contest." She looked up at Gabe in sudden concern. "Have you had dinner? You must be starved since you missed lunch." She gasped at the allusion. The lunch hour was the last thing she wanted to think about. Her heart lurched as she rushed to cover her blunder. "You had a strenuous day." She groaned softly and bit her lip. This was worse. "I mean—"

"Perhaps Mr. Jackson would like to join us, Caroline." Shiloh had come to stand by her and smoothly put an end to her stumbling.

She took his hand in hers and smiled gratefully at him. He was the cavalry to the rescue. An anchor in the storm, the keeper of her common sense. Oh, Shiloh, she wondered, where were you this afternoon?

"I believe Caroline was worried about your dinner," Shiloh continued, and Gabe knew he was aware dinner had little to do with Caroline's agitation.

"I stopped at a diner by the bridge for a sandwich. I only came in for a cup of coffee."

"Then come have it with us." Shiloh was not ready to let the matter rest. Gabe saw he meant to know what had disturbed Caroline.

"I wouldn't want to intrude."

"No intrusion. I insist." Shiloh took Caroline's arm and led her to their table, leaving Gabe no choice but to follow.

"Caroline?" Gabe remained standing. Shiloh might have been invisible for the notice he paid him.

"Stay. Please," she said huskily. She couldn't look at him. He could throw her into a feverish confusion with just a glance. She wanted him near, wanted to reach out and touch his hard hand and wind her fingers through his. And that, she chided herself, made less sense, particularly after this afternoon.

Acutely aware of Shiloh's thoughtful scrutiny, Gabe took the chair beside her. Leaning back in deceptive ease he was the first to break the lengthening silence. "Good trip, Mr. Butler?"

"Productive." Shiloh studied Gabe unwaveringly beneath hooded lids. "You might say I learned what I wanted to know."

"I thought you might," Gabe murmured. Their gazes met, not clashing, appraising. "Any surprises?"

"Not really," Shiloh said bluntly.

"I see." In other words, Gabe interpreted, nothing in my background disturbed you.

"I still have a question or two that need answers." There was a look of cool determination on Shiloh's immobile face.

Caroline had been silent during the exchange. Concern for Pete and the step he was about to take, and Gabe, warm and sensual, had disrupted her world. She'd listened in preoccupied silence; now she heard the lingering unease in Shiloh. "Should you be back so early if you haven't finished your business?" she asked. "I know you wanted to be here when Pete left for the academy, but he would understand."

"I wouldn't; I promised." Shiloh lifted a hand and stroked the furrows from her forehead. "Stop worrying and smile. I can finish my business here just as well. Better."

"Then I'm glad you came," she admitted.

They lapsed into what seemed to be a desultory conversation. Shiloh questioned, Caroline answered. He spoke only briefly of Pete and then of her work. She responded freely, accustomed to Shiloh's consuming interest. It was a part of their friendship.

"...and Gabe saved me. Again!" Caroline finished her story, making light of her anger, turning the episode at the road into a comic encounter. "It was quite chivalrous, but I was too angry at the time to see."

"Gabe's was a natural reaction, Caroline," Shiloh commented.

"I was in no danger."

"Probably not—at least by your standards. But Gabe didn't know."

"You never did anything like it and you were at the sites dozens of times over the years," she pointed out.

"I sort of eased into it. But given the circumstances I suspect I'd have reacted exactly as he did."

"Yes—" Caroline sighed "—I suppose you would have. You two are amazing. You could pass for brothers. The same coloring, the same size and sometimes ideas seem to flow between you. It's uncanny."

"Are you suggesting we're psychic?" Shiloh's brows lifted, emphasizing the slash of the jagged scar.

"Maybe," Caroline said, a serious note beneath the quick reply.

"Sorry to disappoint you but I've never read a mind in my life," Gabe joined in. He'd been contented to watch and to listen, observing Caroline as she relaxed.

"Neither have I." Shiloh brought his chair down abruptly. "If we seem alike beyond our physical similarities, it's because Gabe and I are two battle-scarred old men who've fought and lived, perhaps to fight again. But I can think of better things to do. This is my first night back home, let's not waste it. What are the chances that I might talk you into dancing with me, little daredevil?''

Caroline laughed. ''Considering that you don't have a dance floor, I'd say the chances were pretty good.''

''That didn't stop Gabe,'' Shiloh pointed out. ''What we need is livelier music. I'll change the tapes and then I'll collect that dance.''

''I worry about him,'' Caroline said as she watched him walk away, winding among the tables. ''He seems such a solitary man. He needs someone in his life.''

''Maybe there is someone,'' Gabe suggested. ''Scotty says he's away almost as much as he's here. Perhaps a woman is part of the reason.''

''No,'' Caroline said surely. ''His travels are only business. If there were anyone he was serious about he would have told me or even brought her to Stonebridge. I'm not a fool, I know he's no saint, but if there's a woman, I pity her. The very fact that she's not his wife is proof he doesn't love her.''

''Have you ever wondered if you might be the reason he has no one in his life?''

''Me?'' Caroline turned an astonished face toward Gabe. ''Of course not. Nothing like that ever entered either of our minds. He was Mark's commander in Vietnam. They were captured together. After his release, when he was able, he came to pay his respects. Stonebridge appealed to him and the inn was for sale, so he bought it. He spends as much of his time here as his other interests allow.''

Gabe listened without interrupting. He could understand how Stonebridge could represent sanctuary for one who'd known the ugliness of death and destruction. Hadn't he felt it himself?

Caroline traced the design of the damask cloth absently and folded her fingers into her palm. "I'd known then for a year that Mark was dead," she said huskily, "and after ten years of waiting and hoping, I wasn't handling it very well. In his own way Shiloh grieved as I did. Perhaps that was our common bond, for we drifted into a friendship that became something very special. He doesn't know I'm aware of it, but he's made himself my champion. He's always here when I need someone. He cares for me, but I could just as easily be his sister. If you think I'm wrong—that he's suffering some unrequited love for me—then you've a lot to learn about Shiloh. He isn't one to suffer in silence. If he wanted me, I'd know it. He's a man with a lot of love to give to the right woman, but that woman isn't me.

"He's a friend, a special friend. No more." She regarded him steadily, her grave gaze meeting his. "Since Mark there's been no one. Until you."

"I know." Gabe covered her hand with his. It was warm and strong. "I think I've known it from the first, but I needed to hear you say it."

"I really don't know what I'm saying. I don't understand what's happening to me."

"To us," Gabe amended softly.

"To us." She nodded. "Today was a mistake."

"Only because it was too soon. We were good together. I'm not a sex fiend, nor a monk. I've had my share of women, but I've never felt as I did with you. Nothing so perfect should be called a mistake."

"It could be."

"No!"

"Yes." She wouldn't be swayed. "For me."

"How? Tell me, how?"

"Our life-styles are too different. We've walked different paths, we need different things from life. All we have in common is this attraction, and as powerful as it is, it's not enough."

"It's a beginning. In time there would be more; we both know it. Caroline—" his hand tightened over hers "—are you afraid of caring for me?"

They both knew he didn't mean simple caring. She closed her eyes and seemed to shrink from the truth. "I can't! I've had that kind of caring once. It was enough."

"It *was* enough, but is it now? Will it be in the future? Don't shut me out yet. Give me a chance. Give us a chance."

"I don't think I can. You could ask too much. After today we both know I couldn't say no." Her voice dropped to a ragged breath, the glimmer in her eyes could have been tears. "You could destroy me, Gabe. You wouldn't mean to, but you could."

"I couldn't. I wouldn't. I'm as new to this as you are. Newer. But I promise you I'll never ask for more than you can give."

"And if what I can give isn't enough?"

"Then I'll settle for it. My sexual encounters have been like my life: hard and fast, with no strings attached. Until today, when I found something I've never known before, something precious. I won't deny that I'd like nothing better than to sweep you from that chair and carry you to my room and love you as you've never been loved before. I want to discover if

the magic is real, if it can last.'' He stopped short at
her look of alarm. "But I won't, Caroline," he murmured soothingly. "I don't know what the future
holds. For now, we won't think about it. We'll start
again at the beginning and go forward, one day at a
time."

"Can we?"

"A day at a time, that's all I ask. No more."

Hope stirred then: the essence of strength that had
made her the woman she was; the courage that could
challenge fear and embrace the dream that might be.
To live without hope was to walk in darkness, and her
life had been dark for too long. Understanding that
hope was a wish, not a promise. Caroline smiled—not
her wicked, mischievous smile, but tremulously, with
her heart in her eyes.

"Sorry I took so long." Shiloh loomed over them,
his gaze not missing their clasped hands. "One of the
guests has a complaint that only I can settle. I'll be a
while."

"No problem," Gabe said easily. "Caroline was
just about to tell me more about herself."

"I was?"

"Yes." Gabe was vaguely aware that as Shiloh
moved away he chuckled under his breath. It was a
mocking sound, as if he knew Gabe had just con-
signed himself to the particular hell of wanting and
waiting.

"Why was I going to do that?" she asked.

"Because I want to know you better."

"Where do I begin?" She frowned as she pondered
what she would share with Gabe.

"Begin with Mark," Gabe said in an expressionless
voice.

The more
you love romance . . .
the more
you'll love this offer

FREE!

Mail this heart today! (See inside)

**Join us on a Silhouette® Honeymoon
and we'll give you
4 free books
A free manicure set
And a free mystery gift**

IT'S A
SILHOUETTE HONEYMOON —
A SWEETHEART
OF A FREE OFFER!

HERE'S WHAT YOU GET:

1. Four New Silhouette Desire® Novels — FREE!

Take a Silhouette Honeymoon with your four exciting romances — yours FREE from Silhouette Books. Each of these hot-off-the-press novels brings you the passion and tenderness of today's greatest love stories . . . your free passports to bright new worlds of love and foreign adventure.

2. A compact manicure set — FREE!

You'll love your beautiful manicure set — an elegant and useful accessory to carry in your handbag. Its rich burgundy case is a perfect expression of your style and good taste — and it's yours free with this offer!

3. An Exciting Mystery Bonus — FREE!

You'll be thrilled with this surprise gift. It will be the source of many compliments, as well as a useful and attractive addition to your home.

4. Money-Saving Home Delivery!

Join the Silhouette Desire subscriber service and enjoy the convenience of previewing 6 new books every month delivered right to your home. Each book is yours for only $2.24 — 26¢ less per book than what you pay in stores. And there is no extra charge for postage and handling. Great savings plus total convenience add up to a sweetheart of a deal for you!

5. Free Newsletter!

You'll get our monthly newsletter, packed with news on your favorite writers, upcoming books, even recipes from your favorite authors.

6. More Surprise Gifts!

Because our home subscribers are our most valued readers, we'll be sending you additional free gifts from time to time — as a token of our appreciation.

START YOUR SILHOUETTE HONEYMOON TODAY — JUST COMPLETE, DETACH AND MAIL YOUR FREE-OFFER CARD

Get your fabulous gifts ABSOLUTELY FREE!

MAIL THIS CARD TODAY.

PLACE HEART STICKER HERE

GIVE YOUR HEART TO SILHOUETTE

Yes! Please send me my four Silhouette Desire novels FREE, along with my free manicure set and free mystery gift as explained on the opposite page.

NAME _____
        (PLEASE PRINT)

ADDRESS _____ APT. _____

CITY _____ STATE _____

ZIP CODE _____ 225 CIY JAYA

Prices subject to change. Offer limited to one per household and not valid to present subscribers.

SILHOUETTE BOOKS "NO-RISK" GUARANTEE

— There's no obligation to buy — and the free books and gifts remain yours to keep.

— You pay the lowest price possible and receive books before they appear in stores.

— You may end your subscription any time — just write and let us know.

START YOUR
SILHOUETTE HONEYMOON TODAY.
JUST COMPLETE, DETACH AND MAIL YOUR
FREE-OFFER CARD.

If offer card below is missing, write to:
Silhouette Books, 901 Fuhrmann Blvd., P.O. Box 9013, Buffalo, N.Y. 14240-9013

"Yes," Caroline agreed. Mark, the beginning and the end of her life. *Until Gabe*, a small voice reminded, but she silenced it. "I met him when I was fifteen, a motherless tomboy attending her first Harvest Ball, discovering for the first time that being a woman could be a wonderful thing. Mark was in his last term at the academy, nineteen, older than the average because of a year spent in the Orient. And from that night there was no one else for either of us."

"Love at first sight."

"Yes. We were so young neither of us ever doubted we'd live forever." There was a sad, but not self-pitying smile on her lips as she continued matter-of-factly. "We planned to marry when I finished my schooling, but a little matter of a war interfered. Mark was fulfilling his military obligation and I was in my first year at the university when we learned he was to be shipped out. We had three days together, then he was gone."

Gabe's hand left hers. His fingers splayed across the taut cords of her neck and his thumb stroked the line of her jaw. His fingertips were comforting. His interest was total as he absorbed every syllable of every word. Caroline looked at him and saw tenderness.

"What are you thinking?" she asked.

"How lucky Mark was to be the first man in your life, to be the one you looked at with the wonder of new love in your eyes. Did he know how fortunate he was?"

"I was the fortunate one." Caroline broke off, shook her head, then concentrated on the water glass she turned endlessly on the table. It was patently clear she wouldn't continue.

Gabe realized this was Caroline's story, not Mark's. She rarely spoke of him, and then only when it couldn't be avoided. "Did you complete your first year at the university?" he prompted, drawing her back from her thoughts.

"There was less than a semester, it would have been foolish not to finish. It was a way to spend the lonely days."

"You didn't return for your second year?"

"No, by then Pete was well on his way."

"Did you never want to go back?"

"I had every intention of returning as soon as it was practical, but circumstances seemed to conspire against it."

"How so?" Gabe's fingers were still, but Caroline was exquisitely aware of his touch.

"My father was ill. He became more and more dependent until he needed me desperately. I couldn't leave him, so I settled for an associate degree in business from the community college. It was enough."

"Did you never wish things had been different? That Pete hadn't been quite so precipitous and you could have exerted more control over your own life?"

"Never. Because of Pete, Mark will never be completely lost to me." She paused. Such conversations were rare, but her thoughts seemed to flow into words at will. Caroline turned from her blank perusal of the pristine white tablecloth.

Gabe felt her tremble and saw in her an aching resignation. He slid his hand down her arm and held her hand. "And so the world lost a gifted architect. It's a crime for your talent to be wasted."

"I have clients. Friends and acquaintances of my father know that from him I acquired an education no university could equal, that I lack only the formal endowment of the credentials.''

"You're happy with that?''

"Very. I have as much business as I want and sometimes more.''

"And personally? Are you happy?''

"I've been content.''

Julie's laughter preceded her as she stepped into the dining room with Shiloh close behind. Caroline realized with a start that the tables were empty. It was time for the dining room to close. As she slipped her hand from Gabe's, she was glad for the respite. She faced the newcomers eagerly. "We thought you'd deserted us.''

"I did try to convince Shiloh to run away with me.'' Julie grinned and shrugged. "No luck.''

"She's being modest,'' Shiloh drawled. "I offered her castles in Spain and all my worldly goods if she and the babe would come away with me, but her heart belongs to Kevin.''

Gabe chuckled, realized that in the course of the evening he'd begun to see Shiloh in a new light and started to understand his friendship with Caroline. For beneath the tough, rakish exterior was a man who truly liked women. Judging from his concern for Pete and his teasing appreciation of Julie's pregnancy, Gabe suspected Shiloh was more than fond of children.

"What time will Kevin be here, Julie?'' Caroline asked.

"He won't. Tonight I'm walking. We need the exercise.''

"I'll drive you,'' Gabe and Shiloh said at once.

"You've been overruled." Caroline chuckled. "Better go voluntarily, or I suspect someone will carry you to a car."

"Ha! Remember I outweigh you all." Julie was enjoying the exchange, but the others saw that she was tired. Fatigue showed in the dark circles beneath her eyes. She was in the act of sitting when the pleasant expression on her face vanished. Her eyes were wide, her mouth shaped into an O, her hands folded protectively over the mound of her stomach.

"What is it, Julie? Is it the baby?" Shiloh was instantly by her side.

"No! No, it isn't that. I mean, it isn't the baby. Well, it is the baby, but it isn't." Julie threw her head back in a happy laugh. "I'm making no sense, I know. Here." She clutched at Shiloh's hands and placed them where her own had been. "Feel. There's two of them. Two! We haven't said anything before, we wanted it to be a surprise. But just now, for the first time, I felt two separate babies. Shiloh, can you tell? Can you feel the both of them. Shiloh?"

All eyes were riveted on Julie's abdomen. Gabe and Caroline shared her excitement with laughter, but as he touched Julie's stomach Shiloh seemed oddly moved. Yet in the space of a heartbeat he'd stepped away, a slow smile of utter delight spread over his features. His color returned, only the unsteady fingers that raked through his hair betrayed him.

"Did you see what I mean?" Julie's voice rose in a happy lilt. "After all these years of waiting, and at my age, two! Can you believe it?"

"No, Julie," Shiloh teased, his voice a little husky. "I'd come nearer believing a football team rather than just two."

"Heaven forbid!" Julie laughed. "Kevin may be a coach, but I will *not* supply a team for him. As exciting as it is, at thirty-two the thought of having even one is scary. Sometimes I don't know what I'm going to do."

"What you're going to do right now is get your things and I'll drive you home." Shiloh turned and for the first time, with his guard down, Gabe saw traces of trust in the tired eyes of the gentle renegade. "You'll see that Caroline gets home safely?"

"My pleasure," Gabe promised softly.

Six

The sound of a diesel engine faded and taillights winked out as Shiloh's car rounded a curve on the winding road leading from the inn. Only the palely diffused light from lanterns hung by the flagstone walk softened the darkness.

"A storm brewing?" Gabe looked at the starless sky, then at Caroline who stood by his side.

"Just a cloudy night. There will be fog later, but no rain."

"Then shall we walk?"

"I'd love it."

"Do you need to collect Pete?"

Caroline shook her head a little sadly. "No, one of his older friends has a car now. He'll drop him by later." She sighed wistfully. "It seems that suddenly he's growing up in so many ways."

The moon chose that moment to break through the patchwork of clouds. Its light spilled over the lawn, casting long shadows and turning droplets of moisture that clung to each blade of grass to diamonds.

"Right on cue. Moonlight for our moonlight stroll," Gabe said. Grasping her elbow in a courtly gesture he guided her down the path that followed the meandering stream. Disturbed by their footsteps a frog croaked and hopped away. A faint splash indicated he'd abandoned his foraging on land. "So! It's a nice night for a swim."

"If you're a frog."

"That's not such a bad idea."

"Hmm," Caroline murmured noncommittally.

Gabe hardly seemed to notice as he pursued the conversation. "Some frogs have all the luck."

Small stones crunched under their feet as they walked. Caroline waited for Gabe to continue. She glanced at him and even in the darkness she could read the pretended innocence on his face. It never ceased to amaze her that beneath the sophistication, the jaded worldliness, lurked a wild sense of humor. Well aware that his nonsense was an effort to distract her from her thoughts, she let herself fall into his trap. Stopping by the ghostly skeleton of a fallen tree she folded her arms beneath her breasts and fed him his lines. "Okay. Why is it that some frogs have all the luck?"

"Because they get kissed by beautiful women and become handsome princes."

"For that you'd envy a poor ugly frog?"

"If the beautiful woman were you." He looked into her upturned face. In the moonlight her hair was gossamer, tinted with the fire of auburn, and he could almost believe the gray of her eyes had become lavender.

"But you're already handsome, so you don't need my kisses," Caroline pointed out logically.

"I think I've just been thwarted by a compliment." Gabe chuckled and draped his arm about her shoulder, holding her close as they resumed their walk.

The gloom that had hovered throughout the evening lifted a bit. Her mood brightened, and it seemed a natural thing to have his arm about her. Without thinking she hooked her thumb in the waist band of his jeans. Matching stride for stride they trudged in silence, concentrating on the trail that nearly disappeared as the moon was swallowed by a cloud.

"It's really a matter of opinion," Gabe said, as if launching into the middle of a conversation.

"What matter? Whose opinion?" Caroline asked cautiously.

"Kisses. Yours. Mine."

"Is shorthand another of your languages?"

"Sometimes." Gabe ducked a low-hanging branch and Caroline slipped from his side. He stifled his protest and continued with his nonsense. "Shorthand as a rule is easily interpreted. A key word or two will serve."

"Let me guess—kiss?"

"You're a fast learner." Gabe reached for her.

"Look! My bridge." She danced beyond his grasp.

"You're changing the subject."

Caroline laughed and whirled away. Her running steps beat a rapid tatoo on the wooden floor of the bridge. On the other side she stopped and turned. "Coming, prince?"

"Is that an invitation?"

"It is."

Caroline led him into the darkened room. "Joe's sleeping. If we can get past him without a light he won't wake. There's a lamp by the sofa that never disturbs him, it's little more than a candle."

"What about our voices?" Unconsciously, Gabe whispered conspiratorially although Caroline spoke in her normal tone.

"He's accustomed to Pete's stereo so our noise will be nothing in comparison. The waterfall should mask our footsteps. Just in case, let's go quietly." Catching his hand in hers, she tiptoed by the bird hunched in his cage among the greenery.

Gabe had forgotten how peaceful he'd found her home. It was that rare creation that offered sanctuary for the troubled and rest for the weary. But tonight its effect was the opposite for Caroline. Her mood changed abruptly, as if she found the empty quiet a prelude to loneliness. After she'd waved him to his seat he watched as she in turn sat, stood, paced, then sat again, sinking deeper into her somber thoughts. At last she stood before the window, staring out at the night as if in its passing it offended her.

"What is it, Caroline?" she turned with a look of surprise and he wondered if she'd forgotten him.

"I beg your pardon?"

"Tell me what's bothering you."

"It's nothing."

"A pretty disturbing 'nothing', I'd say." The world had tumbled in on her today. A part of it was what they'd shared, but there was more. More even than the natural concerns of a mother whose son was growing up and away from her, Gabe thought.

"Why would you say that?"

"For one thing, you've been pacing the floor like a caged animal."

"I'm sorry. I didn't mean to be such miserable company. Can I get you something? A drink, anything?"

"Caroline." It was a gentle command, silencing the flow of words she used to hide her distress. "Come, sit down and talk to me."

With a surprising meekness, she came to him and Gabe tucked her neatly, comfortably, beneath his arm. "Now, tell me what this is all about," he said. "And don't say 'nothing.' Spare me that."

"I think you know."

"Pete?"

She nodded, not trusting herself to speak.

"I don't quite understand?"

"I know," she sighed. "I don't, either. For weeks now, I've been bouncing back and forth like a yo-yo."

"About the academy?"

"One minute I feel wonderful about it, then the next I worry that I've made a mistake. For years Pete and I have planned for the day he would enter the academy. He's always seemed to be eager to go, but now I wonder if it's what he really wants, or does he want it for me. Mark's was an old Southern family. Once they'd been wealthy, but gradually that changed and as it did they seemed to cling desperately to the old ways, becoming more and more steeped in traditions. They weren't a military family, but for generations all the young men of the Donovan family spent their prep-school years at Stonebridge Academy. But the family began to die out. Mark had no brothers or sisters, his parents were older, and now there's only Pete. Because he's alone, I suppose I wanted to give him some sense of his family heritage, a sense of belonging—a legacy for the future. Now I wonder if it was my dream and not his. Was I so single-minded he was left with no choice?''

Gabe felt a kinship with the young boy. Hadn't he felt a deep loneliness in knowing that but for himself his own family teetered on the brink of extinction? It was a thought that left one hollow inside. Caroline had strived to counteract that emptiness; she'd given the boy the security of his heritage. A poor substitute for the father, perhaps, but still a precious link. ''Pete seems to be a happy boy.'' Gabe was surprised that his voice was thick with emotion and with pride in the woman beside him. ''I'm sure he's going to miss you, and he'll worry about leaving you alone, but if he'd been unhappy about the school, wouldn't you have seen it?''

''I suppose.''

''And if he's not happy there, is there any reason that he can't withdraw?''

She looked a little startled that there could be the remotest possibility Pete wouldn't have an option. ''No, of course not.''

''Then,'' Gabe suggested gently, ''why don't you accept the fact that you've done the best you could, and leave the rest to Pete?''

''I'm not sure he would be honest, for fear of disappointing me.''

''Leave that to me, or Shiloh. One of us should be able to reach beyond any brave front and find the truth.''

''Why would you involve yourself in Pete's problems?''

"Because I want to be involved. Because he's a fine young man who might not yet realize there's a strength in admitting a problem. Because I like him. Because he's your son. Now, does that set your mind at ease?"

Caroline smiled. "It does, until the next time. We both know I'm going to be plagued with doubt for weeks. But thank you, Gabe."

"He is a fine young man," he repeated, "and a strong one."

"Yes," she murmured, "and even stronger with your help and Shiloh's." The anxiety had eased, the tenseness of her body relaxed and she looked at him, her expression thoughtful. "Is it always so hard for a strong man to accept a weakness? You were a long time admitting the assassin's bullet left you with more than a scar."

"The headaches and vertigo are a thing of the past."

"No. I know you were dizzy today. It didn't last long and you tried to hide it, but for a few minutes, very early this morning, you were pale and a little unsteady."

"It was the first in a very long time, and it was seconds, not minutes," Gabe said reluctantly.

"But it happened."

"Pretty sharp, aren't you?" Gabe hugged her to him, his hand closing about her shoulder.

"I have my days." Her newest worry seemed to melt away at his touch and she leaned against him.

"Don't look for trouble, Caroline. The headaches have stopped and today's vertigo was mild. Soon, except for the scar, the whole thing can be forgotten. I'll be fine and," he added, "so will Pete. Remember, if he won't be open with me, he will with Shiloh."

"You like Shiloh after all, don't you?" She phrased it as a question, but there was no doubt in her. She'd seen it in the look that passed between them, and heard it in their voices as they shared a concern for Julie. It delighted her that the strange undercurrent of wariness might end.

"Like him?" He trailed his hand from her shoulder to her face and pressed her cheek against his heart. There was only the slow, measured rise and fall of his breathing as he weighed what he knew of the man. Despite his aloof restraint, Gabe knew instinctively that Shiloh Butler was a man of integrity. He was a man haunted by something in his past, but an honest one.

"I respect him." Remembering his first encounter with Shiloh and his suspicions, Gabe was faintly surprised at the ease of his admission. Respect? Not quite the whole of it. "Yes," he admitted. "I like him."

"I'm glad." Caroline tilted her head on his chest. Her features were serene, the tumult of her life supplanted by her pleasure. Somewhere deep inside her was born the assurance that Pete would find his way, he would be all right.

What of Gabe? she wondered. He'd come to Stonebridge hurt and a little lost, unaccustomed to the sedate life forced upon him. But he'd adjusted, fitting in as if he'd always belonged. Now he seemed almost content. The dark stubble of a day's growth of beard accentuated the strong jut of his jaw and the softly smiling line of his mouth. The furrows carved by long hours under the baking sun nearly disappeared when his features were in repose.

"You look contented," she murmured.

"I am, but for want of one thing." He smiled.

"And what might that be?"

"A kiss."

"For an ugly frog?"

"For me."

"Then why don't you?"

Gabe's teasing smile faded as he realized the comic whimsy that should have accompanied their routine was missing. In the dusky glow of the solitary light her face was like a delicate cameo. Beneath the shadow of her lashes her gaze was dreamy and unfocused, her lips were parted, soft, moist, a little wistful. She was exquisite, as intoxicating as rare wine. "What?" The word seemed to stop in his throat.

"I asked you why you didn't kiss me." Only the tiny catch in her voice betrayed the quiet desperation that had come upon her like an ambush, transcending fear and worry and all thoughts of tomorrow.

Gabe's eyes met hers. Like crystal pools they captured the frail lamplight, glittering softly. Yet as he searched them they darkened until he was reminded again of a stormy sea—turbulent, sensual. His gaze held hers, probing, riveted, and for an eternity he lost himself in her. Only the slow sweep of her lashes broke the mesmeric trance.

"Less than an hour ago I made a promise." He faltered as she breathed a half sigh that touched him with fire. Gabe, known among his compatriots as a man with a will of iron, felt that legendary control begin to crumble. "I promised..."

"To take no more than I offered," she finished for him. "A kiss, Gabe. Just one. Surely we can allow ourselves that much. A new beginning. We'll go from here and find out together if the magic can last." Her voice sank even lower, an irresistible invitation.

Now his gaze became a blue-hot flame searing into her, reaching into the depths of an awakening passion. He wanted and needed to believe what her waiting stillness told him. And for the first time in his adult life he was unsure.

Caroline caught the leap of uncertainty in his face and with an inherent wisdom she knew that he, too, was vulnerable. For the first time she understood that it might not be she who would be destroyed. Even the strongest could be hurt if the magic he wanted so desperately disappeared. Suddenly it no longer mattered that he represented impermanence, danger, loneliness—everything she'd tried so hard to avoid. It mattered only that she couldn't bear that he might ever be hurt. She touched his cheek and felt the world disappear. There was only Gabe. "One kiss, Gabe. Just one."

"Oh God!" His arms wound about her, drawing her so closely against him that she felt he would take her into himself. Then his lips were warm against hers. Tender. Hungry. Urgent.

There was a fettered wildness in him, she could feel it. Her fingers threaded through his hair as her lips parted beneath his, responding.

"Caroline," he muttered as he kissed her, his mouth hard against her in a need that couldn't be gentle. Far too soon, and with a shuddering sigh, he released her mouth, his lips trailing over her smooth skin. Then, burrowing his face in her hair, he held her. His breathing was harsh, the beat of his heart ragged.

She could feel the blood pounding through him. It was matched by her own as she kissed the pulse at the hollow of his throat. With her tongue she tasted the clean saltiness of his skin, and in an indrawn breath

savored his male fragrance. Her sigh of pleasure
fanned his fevered skin.

Gabe reeled from the impact. Despite the heated
desire and the passion reborn between them, this
guileless caress freely given drove him further from
sanity. In a swift move he swept her from her seat,
settled her on his lap and captured her chin in his
palm.

Bewildered by his kisses and by her own responses,
Caroline stared up at him. She was too bemused to see
the change in his expression from incredulity to
triumphant satisfaction. There was no time to think as
his mouth came down again on hers. This kiss was
only a brief caress, over quickly but no less won-
drous. Somewhere in the back of her mind she knew
there was a thing she should think about, should remember. But not just yet, not while Gabe's lips were
only a heartbeat away. Barely conscious that she lifted
her body that infinitesimal distance, she melded her
mouth with his.

Desire consumed her. Driven by a nameless hunger
she caressed him as he had caressed her and touched
him like a lover. Her mind might never remember this
moment with any clarity—but her heart would not
forget. Tucked away inside would be the memory that
he trembled in her arms.

Gabe tried with a last vestige of strength to draw
away but her cry of loss defeated him. He had risen
mindlessly with her in his arms and taken the first
steps down the hallway that would lead to the bed-
rooms when he stopped, a franticness marring his
usual grace. "No!" he groaned softly as he struggled
with his madness. His arms tightened about her, his
cheek rested against her hair. "No. No. No." The

word repeated over and over became a desperate litany. "Forgive me."

His desperate apology penetrated Caroline's befuddled mind like a dash of cold water. What had been a hazy dream was chillingly clear. She'd given herself to the rapture of his lovemaking with no concern for where it might lead. He had only to touch her and she became an amnesiac, forgetting everything except Gabe. Leaving the burden of reason to him she'd led him to the edge. Her inexperience and disgusting naiveté were poor excuses. She damned her own foolishness, and every nerve in her cried shame as she stiffened in his arms. "Please put me down."

Slowly, carefully, he did as she asked.

"Gabe?" She put her hand on his arm and hurt inside when she felt him flinch. In the shadows she could see only the massive lines of his body when she needed so much to see his face. Silhouetted against light she saw his fist clench in a gesture she interpreted as anger. "I don't blame you for being angry. I should have understood when I kissed you like a wanton that a man of your experience would . . ."

"Shh." Gabe laid his hand over her mouth to stem her flurry of apologies. "In the first place, I'm not angry. I haven't any right. I broke a promise."

"But you didn't!" This time only one finger slanted over her lips, effectively sealing them.

"Hush, Caroline. No more excuses. Will you hear me out?" He waited for her nod before he took his finger away. When he continued it was as if the interruption hadn't occurred. "In the second place, you're anything but a wanton, and I'm anything but experienced with a woman like you. Lastly, we've both apologized, but there's nothing for either of us to for-

give. The fault lies in underestimating the power of
what's between us. When we made love in the meadow
today, you became a fever in my blood. I'm not sure
it can be cured or controlled. So we have to be even
more careful than we realized." The touch of his finger again against her lips was like a kiss, and she
trembled.

"Caroline, don't." He drew his hand away swiftly.
"Don't look at me like that." He closed his eyes in an
effort to shut her lovely image from his mind. "Do
you know that despite all my brave words and high-
flown promises I still want you, here, now, this minute?"

"I know," she whispered.

"I'm not sure any promise I make you is worth a
tinker's damn. Does that frighten you?"

"No," she replied and felt no guilt in the lie.

"Pete should be home soon, shouldn't he?"

"Any minute."

"I think I'm grateful for that."

"Yes," she agreed fervently, touching his hand,
barely suppressing a shiver as it engulfed hers. "Come
back to the sofa and I'll get you a drink."

"The strongest you have."

"That would be Scotty's dandelion wine." Eager to
leave the subject of wanton kisses and fault, she seized
on his suggestion with the sense of mischief that had
always served her so well.

"Scotty's? Do I dare?"

"Be brave. I've survived it." Her wobbly grin was
a welcome sight as she disappeared into the kitchen.

After she'd gone, Gabe pondered the changes that
had taken place in his life in the past weeks. Absently
he returned to the sofa and took his seat. With his feet

crossed one over the other and his fingers laced at the nape of his neck he stared at the ceiling. A low chuckle began, then became a quiet laugh.

"Chimney fires, yellow raincoats and sooty firemen, bulldozers and picnics, love in the meadow, and dandelion wine! What next?" he wondered aloud.

"Gabe!" Caroline stuck her head through the doorway. "Would you prefer Scotty's gooseberry wine?"

He turned unbelievingly, then convulsed once more into laughter. He started to speak and laughed harder. He managed a wave of his hand meaning yes, no, anything, I surrender.

"Well," Caroline drawled, "I hadn't realized that gooseberry wine was so funny. I only offered it because it's not quite so strong. But since you insist on the dandelion, I think I'll find the oldest bottle."

"Heaven help me," Gabe gasped as she ducked back into the kitchen. The sudden realization of how often he'd made that particular plea since meeting Caroline was accompanied by a fresh spate of laughter.

"I hope you're calmer now." Caroline eyed him warily as if she expected him to break into guffaws at any time.

"Oh, I am, I assure you," Gabe answered gravely, hiding another chuckle.

"You don't look calm."

"I don't?" With theatrical care he composed his face into a dignified mask and gave her a solemn look that failed to hide a sparkle of mirth. "Better?"

"Not much."

"Sorry. It's the best I can do."

"Never mind." Caroline knew when she was defeated. She poured a clear liquid into two tulip glasses. Taking one for herself she offered the other to Gabe.

"It's not yellow."

"Of course not."

"The flowers are."

"Drink your wine, Gabe."

"First a toast."

"Stalling?"

"Wouldn't you?"

Caroline only grinned. Wickedly.

"My toast." He touched his glass to hers. "To laughter and kisses. And to love."

Love! Her heart lurched at the forbidden word. The glass slipped through her fingers. The potent liquid spattered over the carpet seconds before the glass splintered against the edge of the table. She stared mutely at Gabe.

Help! Help! He got me. Help!

"Joe!" Caroline was on her feet, the spilled wine and broken glass ignored as she rushed to his cage, less in concern for the startled bird than in an effort to escape the dread and hope that entwined as they waged a battle that left her breathless.

Gabe was bemused by her reaction to his toast and by himself for proposing it. It had been an impulse. Listening as she soothed the startled parrot, he knew he would find no answers to his behavior tonight. Resignedly he sank to his knees and began to pick slivers of glass from the carpet.

"Chimney fires..." He shook his head as he recalled his recitation. "And the bird. How could I forget the bird?" With a groan he applied himself to the search for the smallest splinters of crystal.

The soothing cadence of Caroline's voice was punctuated with growls and squawks. Joe's feathers were ruffled and his glare impossibly bright. He ducked his head and set his perch in motion, whimpering as it swayed. Gabe almost felt sorry for him. It must have been frightening to be awakened from a deep sleep by the crash of breaking glass. The swinging perch served to soothe the bird. He grew quieter, and Gabe began to have hopes for the remainder of the evening.

Gimme a beer.

"I should have known," Gabe muttered. He stood slowly, picked up his own full glass, speculated about its contents and decided that perhaps he owed Joe a vote of thanks, after all. He was smiling as he walked to the kitchen to dispose of the wine—and headed for the apple juice.

As Caroline had predicted the clouds had become an opaque fog that clung to the land. Gabe was wrapped in it as he retraced his path. Carefully walking unfamiliar ground, he was grateful for the moon. Although its light was blurred it had become his link with the world. His footsteps were oddly muffled and made no sound. No night creatures stirred in the darkness. As he breathed the saturated air he became increasingly aware that in this eerie haze he was undeniably alone. How easy it would be to be swallowed up by this cocoon of white, to become disoriented as it erased every landmark. Caught in this faceless land, would it be as easy to lose touch with reality?

"You're getting fanciful, Gabe." As he turned his attention to the trail he couldn't see, reality became the sound of rushing water. He kept the creek constantly to his right, secure in the knowledge that it would lead him eventually to his destination.

He needed total concentration to guide his footsteps, but thoughts of Caroline intruded. Once she'd been alone, perhaps as lost in a fog as he was now, and as he did, she'd found something to guide her. The drive to answer Pete's needs had become the focus of her life, the purpose that had sustained her in the long years of waiting. When the waiting ended, leaving her bereaved and hurt, she locked a part of herself away from the world. In the weeks he'd known her, that protected part had begun to emerge, almost against her will. She had reached out to him. For a while he had held her, touched her and made love to her, but he had not truly breached the wall that contained her. Could he?

And what is it I truly hope to find there? It was an unanswerable question—like all the others he'd asked himself.

The swirling mists parted and the inn loomed before him. His answers wouldn't be so easily discovered. But when they were, they would determine the direction of his life. They would be the foundation of all his tomorrows.

His steps were surer as he crossed the footbridge and climbed a sloping hill. The fog again clung thickly at its crest but he had the glimmering radiance of the inn's lanterns to guide him. The land grew less rugged, thick grass cushioned his feet. He recognized the shape of the giant oak that shaded the veranda. As he stepped beneath its branches he knew he was not alone. With almost a sixth sense, he felt the weight of a stare boring into him. He slowed his pace, halted.

Leaves rustled wetly, a stone shifted and Shiloh stepped out of the mist. "Is she all right?" His voice was deadened and curiously hollow, stifled by the heavy air.

"She will be."

"She's quite a woman."

"Yes."

A match flared briefly. Cupping his hands about it, Shiloh shielded the faint glow with his palms as he lit a cigarette. It was a move of stealth, unnecessary in the quaint village of Stonebridge. A telling move.

"There's no danger here, Shiloh."

"Old habits." He shrugged and smiled ruefully. "They die hard." The match was dropped and crushed in the dust. Shiloh had the look of a man who'd come to a decision. "It's time we talked."

"My room," Gabe suggested.

"My apartment," Shiloh countered. "I have a bottle of cognac that should suit the occasion."

"Anything, as long as it's not dandelion."

"You too?"

"Almost. Joe distracted Caroline and I seized the opportunity to pour it down the drain."

"You owe Joe one. I wasn't quite so lucky." Shiloh chuckled as he turned to cross the lawn.

In five minutes the men were seated across from each other, glasses of cognac before them. Shiloh picked up a folder from a table and tossed it to Gabe. He thumbed through it slowly, scanning it lightly. He was exceptionally familiar with the subject matter. He made no comment as he put it aside.

"Gabriel Kent Jackson. Thirty-eight, no living family, no romantic entanglements. Veteran, engineer of extraordinary skill. Known to perform certain

services for the State Department. Wounded by ter-
rorist in Saudi. Extended medical leave." Shiloh
watched him over the rim of his glass. "Anything
missing?"

Gabe glanced briefly at the folder that described
dates, places and people in minute detail, then back at
Shiloh. "Not unless you have a burning desire to know
that I had my teeth cleaned three days before I came
to Stonebridge.

"That little piece of information came today by
telephone." He picked up the dossier and replaced it
in its original location. "I should imagine you've been
as curious about me. For Caroline's sake."

"And for mine." Gabe said flatly. By rote, in
clipped half sentences, he began to repeat the information Sam Danton had garnered. "Shiloh Butler, a
child of Southern aristocracy, heir to too many business concerns to be enumerated. By avocation an ar-
tisan of metals—a blacksmith, if you wish. Ace pilot
in Vietnam. Captured, imprisoned for ten years. A
year in military hospitals to recuperate. And then
there's Stonebridge and Caroline."

"I'm sure you realized long ago that she's special to
me, that it goes beyond mere friendship."

Gabe nodded.

"It's a long story."

"When it comes to Caroline I have forever."

"I suspected as much," Shiloh said. He rested his
hand against his forehead and with his thumb mas-
saged his temple. His face was drawn and haggard in
the light.

Gabe wondered how badly his head ached, and just
how much agony his eye caused him. Of necessity, in
the isolation and primitive conditions that frequently

accompanied his work, he'd gained more than a smattering of medical knowledge. He knew of damaged optic nerves, and of pupils that failed to adjust to changing light. He'd witnessed the lasting pain of such injuries. It was little wonder the man often seemed morose and withdrawn.

Gabe stood, gathered up his glass and Shiloh's. At the bar he splashed a generous portion of brandy into each. After setting Shiloh's glass at his elbow, he resumed his own seat. Sipping the cognac, he waited.

Seven

—

Mark and I served together in Vietnam." Shiloh's voice cut through the stillness. He wearily touched his scar, then curled his fingers around the arm of his chair. The tenseness in his jaw was the only betrayal of his pain. There were no others visible to the untrained observer, yet Gabe saw and was patient.

"We also shared a little corner of hell." The words grated harshly on the ears of his listener, but Shiloh seemed unaware of it as he dredged up dark memories.

"You and your crew flew one of the secret missions that went wrong." Gabe hazarded a guess.

Shiloh's short bark of laughter held no humor. "It went wrong, almost from its inception, but we were committed, we had no choice. It was a gamble we had to take. Because of the low probability of success, with one exception the crew were volunteers. One man was not given the choice. Mark Donovan had certain rare skills that might have made the mission a success if anything could. Of all my regrets the greatest is that the one man who had no say was the man we lost.''

"You were shot down."

"Yes."

"Was Donovan killed in the crash?''

"Oh God, no," Shiloh groaned. "We spent ten long years in the filthiest, most inhuman..." He shuddered and leaned his head against fists he clenched before him. Great heaving breaths rattled through the room. "No, dammit! He didn't die then, it couldn't be that easy. I wish it had been. You'd have to know Mark to understand. He was a man who met life head-on. What he couldn't conquer, he turned into a joke. But the deprivation, the starvation, the diseases were something else.''

"I doubt any of you got off lightly," Gabe said.

"Hardly. But for Mark it was worse. His joints were swollen, his body wasted. Every move was painful. But he had a way of sealing off the pain, of forgetting what was happening to him. As he grew sicker and weaker, he lay on one of the filthy pallets that served as our beds, whispering endlessly. At first we were sure his mind had snapped, then slowly the words began to make sense. He was talking about Caroline.

"It was always the same. Caroline was his talisman, and eventually, as we came to know her through him, she became ours. The one ray of hope we had was in the hours we sat listening to him. None of us ever tired of hearing it—what she looked like, the things she did, how she laughed. Mark kept us from despair with his stories of Caroline. He kept himself alive with the promise that one day he'd see her again and make up for the lost years.''

"But he didn't make it."

Shiloh shook his head, his hands were clutching the arm of the chair. "No. He grew even weaker and there was no hope of medical aid. On a cold, wet day, the worst any of us had ever known, he gave up. He said her name once, then turned his face to the wall. We never heard him speak again. It was three more months before his heart stopped, but Mark died that day."

"How much longer was it before you were released?" Gabe felt the bitterness on his tongue.

"One week."

"One week," Gabe said softly. "He almost made it."

"Almost." Shiloh whispered the word, but its bleak uselessness seemed a cry of despair.

"The rest of you survived?"

"In one condition or another. None good. But what we were we owed in part to Mark, and to Caroline. I made a promise that some day I would meet her. I would see for myself..."

"If she was the woman Mark created for you," Gabe supplied when Shiloh seemed at a loss for words.

"Yes."

"And you weren't disappointed?"

"Never." Shiloh murmured. "I came to offer condolence, and found a friend, and a home."

"So you bought the inn, because Stonebridge offered something you needed, as well as to be near Caroline, should she needed you."

"I do what little she'll let me. She's an independent lady. She's had to be."

Gabe looked at Shiloh shrewdly. "You love her."

"Yes, I do."

"But you're not *in* love with her."

"No." He shook his head slowly as if the slightest move were painful. "She was the light in our bleak lives, the laughter we never heard, a dream."

"All the more perfect for her faults," Gabe ventured.

"We were the living dead. She was life."

The goddess of survival, worshipped, protected, kept safely on her pedestal, Gabe added silently. He looked into a brilliant, haunted gaze and knew he was right.

"And you?" Shiloh asked in a low voice.

Gabe held that bright gaze a moment longer, then looked away, staring into the shimmering liquid in his glass. "I don't know," he said after a long silence. "I wish I did. I've been many places and done many things. And there have been women."

"But none like Caroline."

"No. None like Caroline."

"You were vulnerable. You were overworked, tired, a little jaded, and not completely recovered from a horrifying wound. Suddenly you were mortal and your exciting life was less than exciting and very empty. Then there was Caroline—vibrant, alive. All the things you'd missed. Is that how it goes?" Shiloh asked.

"Something like that."

"A provincial little town, a provincial woman. Exciting for their very difference. A passing fancy?"

"You know better," Gabe snapped, fighting a sudden surge of anger, for he knew the point Shiloh was making. Hadn't he faced it himself? Amid grand promises that he wouldn't hurt her, hadn't he told himself that he would stay, that he would unravel the mystery of this fascination—and then leave. Until the meadow, he had thought he'd meant those words. Until those stolen moments that had changed his life, and Caroline had fled—striking fear in him with her doubt. 'A passing fancy? No, she was far more than that.

"Have you ever had an enduring relationship?" Shiloh interrupted his thoughts. "The kind that binds you, ties you down?"

Gabe's answer was a derisive laugh. If he had, this conversation wouldn't need to take place. And Caroline wouldn't be in his life.

"Caroline's been alone too long already. She doesn't need an on-again, off-again affair."

"Dammit!" Gabe's anger spilled over. "Don't you think I know that!"

"When the days and months turn into years and the familiar becomes drudgery, will what you feel for her be enough to hold you?" Shiloh continued calmly.

"God help me, I don't know." Gabe's outburst subsided. "Aren't you rushing things a bit? Maybe I don't know what I feel for Caroline, but the biggest question is what she feels for me. Has it occurred to you that she might not want a rolling stone, even a re-formed one."

"She might not have admitted it, but she wants you."

"Sexual encounters aren't always love," Gabe retorted in an inadvertently revealing answer.

"No, not always." Shiloh was thoughtful. He'd suspected that Gabe and Caroline had become lovers. Now he was sure. For once he couldn't protect her; she'd moved beyond his reach. If an affair with Gabe was a mistake, it was hers to make. He could only watch and hope. But he knew now that if there was pain, it would be Gabe's as well. The man didn't know it yet, but he was caught, ensnared by the innocent enchantment Caroline had woven about him. Those far-flung assignments would intrigue no more, their excitement paling before what he'd found in her. But her loyalties were old, they ran true and deep. Could she put them aside, even for a man like Gabe? Only she knew the answer. Suddenly Shiloh was as concerned for Gabe as for Caroline.

"Go carefully, Gabe," he said at last. "For both your sakes."

"As carefully as I can."

Shiloh lifted his glass. "To Caroline," he said, drinking deeply.

"To Caroline," Gabe echoed.

The bottle of cognac was nearly empty when the clock struck midnight. Shiloh glanced at his watch in surprise, then reached for the telephone. "It's getting late, I think I'll check on her."

He dialed three digits, stopped, turned, and extended the receiver toward Gabe. "I suppose this should be your privilege now."

The significance of the offer was not lost on Gabe. As much as he would like to hear her voice once more, he knew what she needed. He declined the offer with a shake of his head. "No, you call her. I suspect that what she wants more than anything right now is the voice of a comfortable friend."

A small smile curled Shiloh's lips. His disquiet was tempered by a growing respect for Gabe, the man, and his insight. In a matter of seconds he was speaking words of assurance into the telephone.

The sun had hardly risen when Gabe's car slid to a halt in the cluttered yard of his cabin. Even as the door shut behind him he was taking the steps two at a time. The sound of hammering stopped him short in the open doorway. Dressed in jeans and a cotton shirt, Caroline was at the top of a ladder canted against the railing of a balcony. He took a deep breath of relief and stepped into the room, watching and admiring her skill as she pounded a slat into place. When she hooked her hammer in the loop at her belt he spoke. "So here you are."

Caroline half turned toward him, her features showing no surprise, only curiosity. Carefully taking a nail from her mouth she asked, "Where else would I be?"

"I drove by your house thinking you would be there." Gabe frowned up at her. "Why on earth are you here? Today of all days?"

"You did hire me for this job, and this is a workday. In fact, Scotty and the boys should be arriving soon."

"What about Pete?"

"All delivered and settled." She began to step down the rungs. "Assembly was this morning at five. Parents are barred from the proceedings. After I dropped him off I had nothing else to do so I came on out here. I've been wondering for weeks if the loft could be salvaged, and today seemed as good a time as any to find out." She jumped agilely to the floor.

"You were up late last night. You should go back home and rest." Gabe advanced a step.

"You sound like Shiloh." Caroline grimaced and shook her head.

"If I do, it's because both of us want what's best for you. You do need the rest, you know. You can't have had much sleep." He touched the tender flesh beneath her eyes. "These circles prove my point."

"So, I'm an old hag now, am I?"

"Hardly. But you are a woman who's tired."

"That's just the problem. I'm not tired. At least, not tired enough." The nail had been shoved into her pocket, her hands at her hips were tightly clenched. It was clear that she was on edge and fighting it. "I'm going to miss Pete, and I may dither and doubt as I did last night. But right or wrong, and whatever the reason, attending Stonebridge Academy as his father did is the most important thing in his life. I won't wreck it for him. So I'll work it out. For as long as it takes I'll bury myself in this job and leave as little time as possible to think. I'll grow accustomed to being without him. I have to. Until that time—" she waved her hand toward the interior of the cabin "—there's this. It's my way, Gabe. The only way."

"Okay, Caroline." He unbuttoned his shirt at the wrists and began rolling up his sleeves. "If that's how it's going to be, then I'll work with you. When you get up, I'll get up. When you work, I'll work. When you go to bed, I'll go to bed."

Caroline watched him, expecting the punch line, needing it to establish a safe boundary. Between them there seemed to be only ridiculous humor or wild, feverish passion. If today ran true it would be no different, and they both knew it. But she was as wary of herself as of Gabe. Last night had taught her she knew little of herself. She'd thought she could be strong and she hadn't been. He'd only to touch her and the strength that had been the mainstay of her life deserted her. Worse yet, his toast to love had thrown her into a panic. She almost shivered now, recalling the spilled wine, the broken glass, the shock.

Love. She'd had it with Mark, only with Mark. It was a once-in-a-lifetime thing; she'd never love again. No. Whatever it was, this mad attraction between them couldn't be love. He'd promised to ask for no more than she could give. Gabe mustn't ask for love.

Misunderstanding her shaken silence, he took her hand and found it cool and stiff. "Hey, don't freeze up on me. That wasn't a proposition, you know, though we know it could easily have been. I just meant that if you intend to work yourself half to death, I'll be with you hour for hour."

"You can't," Caroline protested, finding her voice at last. Concern for Gabe pushed everything from her mind. "You've done too much already. You're supposed to recuperate."

"Caroline, if I recuperate anymore I'll go clear out of my mind. Anyway, the work I'd do wouldn't hurt me, it would simply be a much-needed change of pace."

"You're sure?"

"Positive."

"Okay. You asked for it." She stooped to take a spare hammer from her toolbox and thrust it at him. Gabe might be stubborn, but he wouldn't do anything foolish. "Remodeling houses is a bit different from building dams and airports, but at least no one will be pointing a weapon at you, and if you concentrate, you'll get the hang of it." It was a moment before she realized that for the first time, she'd been able to think of his work and its dangers with something other than horror. It was a step forward, but in what direction?

"I'm sure I will." His grin took on a devilish slant and Caroline was startled again by the boyishness that lurked so near the surface of his rugged exterior. He moved near to whisper conspiratorially, "And I promise not to kiss you, not even once. Unless, of course, you ask me as prettily as you did last night."

For a moment she was speechless, a little dismayed, until she realized how like him it was to face a situation by putting it in perspective, to lighten the grimness with humor. Her answering smile was slow in coming, but bright and filled with easy mischief. "Well, who knows? I just might." At his raised eyebrow she laughed and drew her hammer from her belt. "But right now I have work to do."

Gabe remained perfectly still as she stepped saucily around him. Then he started to follow her progress as she checked a wall here, a window there, tapping in new nails where they were needed. As she bent and stretched, the cotton shirt pulled taut but stayed snugly tucked at her waist. As she strained against the gentle pull, Gabe knew that beneath the clinging fabric her breasts would be naked, caressed, not restrained, by a lacy camisole.

He turned away and the beads of perspiration glistened on his forehead were not from labor.

A half hour had passed when Caroline called for help. It was stupid but she was caught firmly, her hair tangled by a protruding splinter and a nail. The more she struggled the worse it became. Had she been alone she would have pulled herself free, sacrificing a clump of hair, risking a scratch across her cheek. She'd been tempted even now, but she could almost hear the overreactive furor the scratch would cause. Under the circumstances, Gabe's help was the sensible alternative. She called his name louder and he looked up. "Could you help me, please?"

Wordlessly Gabe rose from his kneeling position and moved to stand behind her. His arms circled her as he worked patiently, his fingers tugging gently at the tousled mass. She felt the heat of his body as it touched hers. The crisp, clean fragrance so distinctly his brought a flood of memories, bitter and sweet, threatening the strength of her trembling legs. Relief was like a deep, cool breath of air when he said, "That's the last of it, you're free."

Before she could move, his hands closed over her shoulders and he turned her to face him. For a long while he stared into her upturned face. Then he carefully extracted a wood shaving from her hair, combing it away with his fingers. A fingertip lingered at her temple before trailing over the curve of her cheek to the fullness of her lower lip. "You make it awfully difficult to keep promises," he muttered.

"I know." The hammer she held slipped through nerveless fingers, falling with a thud perilously close to Gabe's foot. She placed her hands at his waist, her palms gliding over the hard surface of his body, slowly, savoring the feel of him.

"Caroline," he warned.

"Shh," she murmured as her hands at last reached his neck, drawing him to her. "I made no promises. Not one."

The feel of her mouth on his was exquisite, delicate. The sweetness went through him like the shuddering power of an electric current, stunning him. Before his arms could enfold her she danced away, a smile on her lips. Only the quickening of her breath was proof that she was no more immune to their attraction than he. He would have reached for her, but she whirled toward the open doorway, straight into Scotty's arms.

"Good morning to ye, Caroline," the little man boomed as he embraced her and kissed her cheek. "It's an early start you've made. The crew will have some catching up to do."

"Not so much, Scotty, and Gabe's here to help." She touched his gray-bearded cheek and stepped through the door to greet her crew.

"Is she all right?" Scotty asked a silent Gabe.

"She's working on it."

"Yeah, working." Scotty bent to pick up the hammer that still lay at Gabe's feet. He looked at it curiously, but made no comment. "She'll drive herself, for sure. We'll have to watch to see that she doesn't wear herself down."

Gabe nodded in agreement.

Scotty tucked the hammer into his tool belt and sighed gustily. "She's a gallant lass."

"I know."

"The day's a-wasting." Scotty clapped him on the shoulder. "Let's go to work."

Caroline leaned over the bridge's railing, watching as the river swirled and twisted. The bridge, with its massive stones and the weathered beams that rose to cover it, had long been her favorite place. Many nights, after the villagers had closed their doors and shuttered their lights, she walked the winding path that led to it. The hours she'd spent listening to the river were countless.

On Pete's first day away her panacea of long gruel-
ing hours on the job had been unsuccessful. Muscles
better forgotten ached and cramped. A new blister in
the palm of her hand stung like vinegar. The knee
she'd banged against a loose board throbbed and
stiffened. Her body cried out for sleep, but her mind
refused. In the darkest part of the night every corner
of her home had echoed with reminders of her son.
Restless and lonely she'd wandered from room to
room, touching the things that were his, missing the
sound of his laughter, until at last she could stand no
more and had come seeking shelter at the bridge.

She had no idea how long she'd stood, staring down
at the water, when a footstep sounded beyond the
light. She whirled toward it. "Shiloh?"

"Not this time. Care for some company?"

"Gabe." She took a deep, trembling breath, then
whispered gratefully, "I think I'd like that."

He stepped out of the darkness and to Caroline he
represented comfort. "How did you find me?"

"Shiloh said you often came here when you were
troubled."

"He knows me well." A whirling breeze stirred over
the water and she shivered as it plastered her thin shirt
to her.

"You're cold." Gabe put his arms about her and
pulled her to him. He held her in his embrace, warm-
ing her until the shivering stopped. "Better?"

"Much," she said shakily.

"Then let's go home." He kept one arm about her
as they retraced the way back. Caroline seemed to have
no need for conversation so he walked with her in silence. At her door he paused, kissed her lightly on the
forehead, then put her from him. "It's late. You

worked far too hard today and you desperately need rest, so I'll say good-night.''

''Are you very tired, Gabe?'' He'd been as good as his word, keeping pace with her all day. She knew he had every reason to be exhausted.

''I've been worse.''

''Would you stay? I don't think I want to be alone.''

''Would you like for me to call Shiloh?''

''No. I'd like to be with you.''

''I'm yours, Caroline. For as long as you need me.'' He gathered her back into his arms.

Her befuddled mind missed the significance of his promise. The sleeplessness of the night before and her day of labor had finally begun to extract their price. She drooped against him and followed trancelike as he led her into the house.

''Stay put. I'll be back in a minute.'' He left her sitting in the den.

Her bedroom was as he expected—clean, spartan. There were no frills, but it was a totally feminine room. It was a room he would find comfortable, Gabe decided, as he snapped on the bedside lamp and folded the coverlet to the foot of the bed.

Her bathroom was equally neat except for a pair of jeans shed in exhaustion and left in a tangle. His own bathroom had a very similar reminder of the rigors of their day.

An inspection of the medicine chest produced a bottle of aspirins and an envelope containing a muscle relaxant. He took one tablet from each. From a dispenser he took a small paper cup and filled it with water. As quietly as he had left her, he returned to Caroline. She was no longer in the chair but stood at the bookcase, a small, framed photograph before her.

Gabe recognized it. He made no comment. Instead he took one of her hands in his, dropping the tablets into it.

"I don't want these." She turned from the picture and extended her open hand.

"You need them." He closed his fingers around hers, making a fist securing the tablets inside.

"I don't like medicine."

"Neither do I, but sometimes it serves a purpose. Tonight you need these. It's obvious from the way you hold your head that your neck aches, and your shoulders are tight." To prove his point he set the cup down and rested his hands on her shoulders. She flinched beneath even that light pressure. "Take them, please, for me."

Caroline was too tired and it would take too much effort to argue. Obediently she gulped the pills and drained the cup. Gabe took it from her and set it down.

"Come, sit until they begin to take effect."

"I'd just hop right back up again. When I'm this restless I prowl like a cat." Caroline laughed ruefully.

"I've done the same myself," Gabe said. "Would you like to talk?"

"About what?" she evaded.

"About Mark. What you're feeling now is as much for him as it is for Pete."

"Mark's dead. He has been for a long time." Caroline's voice broke as she turned her back.

"Not for you, Caroline. You haven't let him go. It won't be over until you stop letting the pain of his loss cripple you. Living hurts, but we do what we must and we go on."

"I've lived my life as I had to," she protested. "There was no other way."

"Yes," Gabe murmured, "but that's changed now. You've changed."

"I've been feeling all day as if my purpose in life is finished, as if Pete would never need me again. But it's not so, is it?"

"He loves you; he'll always need you."

She was barely aware that Gabe had put his arms about her or that she huddled against him. He was silent, not wanting to break the flow of her thoughts. If it helped that he listened, then he would be there for as long as it took.

"He needs me, but in ever-changing ways." Caroline's voice had begun to slur. "Now it's up to me to put my life in order. To reach out to the living."

"Once you reached out to me in a beautiful sunlit meadow. Do you remember, Caroline?"

"Yes. Beautiful." She settled deeper into his embrace. Gabe felt her relax as she succumbed to the tablets.

He gathered her easily into his arms and took her to the bedroom. As he passed Joe's cage, a gruff growl rose from the foliage. Gabe stopped. His voice was even but threatening: "If you value your life, bird, you'll be quiet."

He didn't wait to see the effects of his threat. He put Caroline down at the edge of the bed and, as she sat passively, began to undress her. Like a sleepy child, she moved obediently as piece after piece of her clothing began to fall to the floor.

"Oh dear." She giggled as his hand brushed her breasts while he fumbled in sudden clumsiness in his chore. "I do believe you've gotten me drugged."

"I only gave you one tablet and an aspirin," he muttered, then ducked to occupy himself with her shoes.

"But I only take half a tablet and never with anything else." She rested her head against his shoulder, nuzzled his neck with her nose and giggled again.

"Now she tells me." Gabe swore softly, then sighed as he kissed her cheek and lowered her to the pillow. She was lovely, she was tempting—almost beyond his strength. He swore again, this time not quite so softly, as he tucked the covers firmly beneath her chin.

"Gabe?"

"I'm here, love."

"I'm sorry I'm such an idiot."

"You're not, you're just a little dopey. We'll laugh about it as we tell our grandchildren."

"Grandchildren?" She tried to open her eyes but her lids were weighted and heavy.

"Four of them," Gabe said. "I've decided."

"Does Pete know?"

"I'll tell him."

"After you tell him, are you coming to bed?" The words were muffled as she snuggled into the pillow.

"No, Caroline, not tonight." Tonight, beneath the false tranquility of the tablets, the past loomed too closely, too painfully; a stronger reality than the present. He would wait as he had been waiting. Tonight belonged to Mark. "But soon," he murmured. "I promise."

"Mmm. Soon."

Gabe chuckled as he kissed her. "I don't know if I should be relieved or sorry that you won't remember this conversation tomorrow." He lingered, watching until her breathing was deep and regular, then he turned to leave.

"Gabe?"

"I'm still here."

"I've been sad for a long, long time, haven't I?"

"A long time, but it's almost over now." He realized that she didn't hear him for she was finally truly asleep.

He moved through the house turning out lights and checking doors, assuring himself their locks were secure. As he passed Joe's cage he paused. "Smart bird, you saved your tail feathers for another day. If you value them you'll stay quiet, at least for tonight."

A grumble and a cool stare met his suggestion.

At the desk Gabe paused again; the handsome man in the walnut frame seemed to be looking at him. He touched the picture but didn't pick it up. After a minute his hand moved away. "She's hurting, Mark, but she'll make it."

He turned away, surveyed the room one more time and walked to the door. As he opened it and stepped through, he said quietly, "Good night, Joe."

Eight

———

Hadn't we better call it a day?"

"Crying uncle?" Caroline faced Gabe as she wiped a film of perspiration from her forehead. It was late October, and she had warned him that while the evenings carried the nip of autumn, the days could still be sweltering. Today had proved the point.

"Don't have the word in my vocabulary. My stamina's better now. No more headaches, no more vertigo, not in weeks. But since it's almost six o'clock and the ball starts at eight, I think my suggestion has merit. Scotty and the crew left over an hour ago."

"You're right, of course. I wanted to walk through the village and stop by Shiloh's smithy on the way home." She stepped back, her hands on her hips as she surveyed the nearly completed cabin. Her smile softened. "It's beautiful, isn't it?"

"Very." Gabe's arms found their way naturally around her waist, his hands clasped at her midriff. "In less than two months you've worked a miracle."

"Not me. We. The cabin's been a joint effort." She curled her hands lightly over his as she nestled comfortably back against him, her hair a cloud against the open collar at his throat. "Have you forgotten the pact you made the day Pete entered the academy? You've kept it to the letter. We've accomplished this together."

"I haven't forgotten," Gabe answered. In nearly six weeks Caroline had never mentioned that time. He had worked by her side, watching her deal with the lonely void left by Pete's absence. He'd stood helplessly by, knowing she relived again and again the anguish of losing Mark. Although she didn't speak of it he knew that she had finally faced the truth, admitting that her grief had turned to a fear isolating her from a normal life as effectively as had the harrowing years of uncertainty. Understanding wasn't conquering, but it was a beginning. The protective scars had been ripped open, the wounds laid bare; the excision, painful but necessary, had occurred. She'd given her son all the laughter and joy his father had possessed, and she'd bestowed upon him the heritage. The rest was up to Pete. She seemed confident he would be secure.

Caroline was happy now, her step was lighter, her laughter gayer, and the serenity that had always been there was deeper, gentler, but no longer a necessity for survival. Soon she would be able to challenge life and accept its risks. The healing was almost complete.

The weeks of her valiant struggle had enriched their friendship. Determined that he would not add to the pressures of her life, Gabe had cooled his desires, avoided situations that might spark the madness. Gradually he'd learned that he could touch her, even embrace her, without the heat of passion. There was a newfound pleasure in just holding her, simply, sweetly, as he did now.

He drew her closer. "We've done the labor together, but the idea was yours. Without your plans none of this would have happened. You've given me a home with the comfort of modern conveniences, and preserved its antiquity."

"It was well built. I had good material to work with."

"How old do you think the original cabin is?"

"Don't you know. Ezra had no records?"

"I didn't find any. I know he was born here, but I've no idea when the cabin was built."

"From the look of the masonry, I'd guess it's at least a hundred years old." Caroline stepped out of the yielding circle of his arms to trail her fingers over the uneven bricks of the fireplace. "This pattern of alternating one line with the short side exposed, and the next with the long side, pretty accurately dates it in the nineteenth century."

"With the short side called 'headers' and the long side 'stretchers,'" Gabe added.

"You already know this," Caroline accused.

"I know construction, you're the architect."

"Not quite."

"Near enough." Gabe laid his arms across her shoulders, his fingers were laced at the nape of her neck. With a slight urging he brought her close. "I thank you, Caroline Donovan, for my beautiful home."

Home. The man who'd had no home, needed none, spoke of it now with a throb of pride in his voice. Caroline couldn't reply, but her head lifted in welcome as his lips came down on hers. It was a gentle kiss, a token of thanks shared between friends. Recently Gabe had done no more than hug her or kiss her cheek. She'd grown comfortable and content with him. Her fear of caring had receded with the contentment and now, with his mouth so undemanding on hers, she found she wanted more. His touch awakened familiar urgency. Her lips parted and her arms closed about him even as he was moving away.

"We're going to be late." He touched her cheek with the back of his hand.

"I know."

"You wanted to see Shiloh."

"Yes, I do."

"Then you have to dress for the ball."

"Obviously."

"Your costume probably has hundreds of buttons."

"I've never counted, but probably."

"It'll take hours."

"Perhaps." Caroline looked up at him. "Have you finished?"

"Finished?" He was puzzled.

"Finished convincing yourself not to kiss me again."

"That's not quite what I've been working on." He laughed and ruffled her hair. "Actually, I was working up to making a pass."

"You were?" Caroline eased back. She realized she'd overstepped the invisible lines Gabe had firmly drawn weeks ago. "Your approach sounds a bit negative."

"Don't you recognize reverse psychology?"

"Sorry."

"Ahh, well. All isn't lost. I still have hope. This dress you're wearing tonight, did you say it has a hundred buttons?"

"I didn't say. You did."

"Humor me."

"Maybe fifty."

"Where are these buttons?"

"On my dress."

"Where on your dress?" He was magnificently patient.

"Down the back."

"Who's done the honors in the past?"

"Pete, of course." She grinned, getting his point.

"Then tonight I shall volunteer my services. I'll come by early to help you dress."

"I think I'd be safer with Scotty or Shiloh."

"Let me assure you, no one can do buttons like I can."

"That's what I'm afraid of."

"You know me too well." Gabe's laughter rumbled through the room as he offered her his arm. "Shall we go?"

Gabe had learned that Harvest Festival was a time the people of Stonebridge relished. It was then they stepped back into history. As he strolled the cobblestone streets with Caroline, they were surrounded by visitors attracted in numbers for the event.

"Is festival week always like this?" he asked as he sidestepped a group of eager youngsters who raced to a guardrail, then stood goggle-eyed as they watched the huge waterwheel of the gristmill turn.

"Always. Hi, Harold." Caroline waved to a man in costume who lounged in the doorway of a gray stone building. Today and for the week, it had become the apothecary. Next week it would be the pharmacy again.

"Hi, Caroline. Gabe."

As they moved on, Caroline related the history of Harold Morgan's store. "There's been an apothecary with a Morgan serving as pharmacist since the town was established. The family used to live upstairs, but in time they moved to a house. Harold converted the rooms into offices for a local lawyer."

They passed the candlemaker's, the potter's, the cobbler's—a shoe store at other times of the year— and innumerable taverns. Gabe had seen them all many times, but today Caroline treated him to a smattering of the past of each. The enticing aroma of food wafted from the Stonebridge Tea House. Gabe's hand on Caroline's arm stopped her at its door. "Would you like to go inside? You should have something before the ball."

"Haven't the time. I'll grab a sandwich later."

"Promise." His hand circled her wrist.

"I promise." Capitulation was easier than argument. "We'd better hurry, or Shiloh will be closing."

Caroline was wrong. Dressed in traditional white shirt, white stockings and black breeches fastened at the knee, Shiloh had just pulled an iron bar from his forge. They listened while he spoke to the children about him.

"It's always like this. The children flock to him. He loves them and they sense it," she whispered. "He

should be finished soon. I'll speak to him, then we'll
be on our way.''

When the simple piece he was working on was done,
Shiloh sent it hissing and spitting into the slack tank
to cool. Steam was still curling toward the ceiling when
he smiled at the children and hurried them on their
way. "Hello, you two." He greeted Caroline with the
tweak of an earlobe and grinned at Gabe. "Ready for
the dance?''

"We will be." Caroline stood on tiptoe to kiss his
chin. "But first have you finished with my design?"

Shiloh tapped her nose and asked, "Why wouldn't
I be? Haven't you reminded me often enough that today was the day?''

Gabe glanced curiously at her as she shrugged and
said apologetically, "Sorry, but it's just that it's so
important.''

Shiloh relented in his teasing. "It's done," he said.
"Packaged and delivered earlier this morning.''

"I should have known I could count on you. Gabe
and I will see you at the ball, won't we?''

"Wouldn't miss it.''

"Caroline," Gabe intervened, "we'd better be
going.''

"Sure." She clasped Shiloh's hands quickly in her
own and murmured a low thanks, then turned back to
Gabe.

"What was that all about?" he asked after they had
waved goodbye and were weaving through the growing crowd.

"You'll see." She laughed and to Gabe she was un-
believably lovely.

"I will? Sounds mysterious.''

"No. Only a surprise.''

"For me?"

"Maybe. Ahh. Here's the inn. I'll leave you now to ponder the mystery." With another laugh she was gone, leaving Gabe to smile over her contagious excitement. As he climbed the stairs to his room to dress for the ball.

"You'd better get your exercise in a hurry. You have to go back into your cage before I leave."

Caroline stared vacantly at the bright plumage of the parrot that paced—if the long-taloned waddle could be considered such—back and forth across the room. The green tail swished left, then right, as the yellow head ducked rhythmically in time. Occasionally his toes almost meshed as they turned inward.

She knew she presented an incongruous picture herself, sitting on a long, sprawling sofa, dressed in the overdress and petticoat of a Colonial maiden. She loved the green-gold gown with its lace-filled neckline that skimmed her breasts, then left bare their creamy slope. How elegant she felt as the skirts swayed gently about her hips, sweeping the tops of her delicate slippers. So different from her daily uniform of jeans, practical shirts and sturdy boots.

In her hair she wore a sprig of Queen Anne's lace, its delicate flowers preserved for a time. She wore it as she had to her first ball . . . her first taste of the sheer joy of looking and feeling like a desirable woman.

Caroline looked down at the small silver box that lay in her lap. Tarnished now by time, it shone like dull ebony. One by one she touched the treasures it held: a band of lace and the bare stem of a shattered flower; an academy ring on a broken chain; a dance program, ivory with age; a lock of hair tied with a scarlet ribbon. Her special memories of Mark. For a long time she looked at them, touching, remembering. There had been laughter and tears in their time together; laughter in their loving, tears in the years that followed. She would remember the laughter. Caroline sighed softly—the slow, whispering sound of a breath long held—then gently she closed the box.

When she rose at last to put it away she didn't see the tall figure in the shadow of the doorway; her mind was too filled with this moment with Mark. She would look at the silver box, and at its precious treasures again, but she knew that it would never be the same. Her hand lingered on the worn lid for a moment longer before she turned away.

"Time to go back in your cage, Joe." She spoke to the bird. Her voice was shaky as she blinked back the rush of tears. "Gabe should be here any minute."

"I'm already here," he said from beyond the small bright circle cast by a single lamp. "I knocked. When there was no answer I let myself in."

"I'm sorry—" she cast a glance toward the silver box "—I was . . ."

"You look lovely, Caroline." With his compliment he stopped the needless explanation. "The gown suits you."

"Thank you, kind sir." She curtsied and her smile was real, if a little trembly.

Gabe stepped into view. Like Caroline, he was dressed in keeping with the period for the ball. A coat and breeches of gray and faun, and the ruffled linen of a creamy shirt became him. He paused there, at the faint edge of the light, and Caroline saw again how handsome he was.

As he walked cat-footed across the room, a low growl sounded at his ankle and he looked down at the bristling bird. "Either Joe doesn't like my old-fashioned shoes or this is quite a watchdog. If he had fangs he'd have them bared."

"With a beak like his, who needs fangs." Her voice was steady again and lilting.

"Who indeed?" Gabe dismissed the bird, turning his attention to Caroline. Her cheeks were flushed, her eyes bright, a thread of low-key electricity seemed to race through her. It was from the excitement of seeing Pete for the first time in weeks, subdued by the torrent of her memories. But Gabe saw no hint of sadness.

"Poor Joe," Caroline said. "He misses Pete."

"I'm sure he does, but not half so much as you do."

"Is it still so obvious?"

"Only to those of us who've been with you and have seen you fight the loneliness."

"Pete mustn't see, he mustn't know. I wouldn't want him to worry."

"Shh." Gabe's hand curled over her lips, stopping the anxious flood. For a moment he stroked their velvet softness, then, fingering the tousled curls that touched the hollow beneath her ear, he drew her head to his chest. He held her closely, quietly, his cheek resting on her hair. When she nestled against him, her anxiety ebbing, he murmured softly, "You've met every challenge, fought every battle; what was needed, you've done. You will again.

"If you need me, I'll be there. And Shiloh, and Scotty too." He put her from him, lifting her chin with the tip of a finger. "Smile for me." He waited until she gave him a tiny smile before he kissed her cheek.

"That's my girl. Now, since your buttons are all done, much to my disappointment, I think we should be going."

"My buttons?" For once her mind failed to move as swiftly as his.

"Of course." There was a wicked glint in his eyes that put the lie to the disappointment he pretended.

Suddenly laughter exploded from Caroline. Her arms slid about his waist as she hugged him to her. "Oh Gabe! You're wonderful! You're so good for me, what will I do when you're gone?"

She was still laughing when she stepped away, and Gabe wondered if she had any idea what she'd said. In a sentence she'd told him how impermanent he was in her life. Was it what she wanted, or what she thought he intended? Could she accept so easily that one day he wouldn't be a part of her life? Pain flickered in him like a small, suffocating flame.

"Before we go, I have something for you," Caroline said. "I have to go to New Orleans tomorrow. Maybe I should have waited until I get back, but I can't. Instead I rushed poor Shiloh. He'd been working on it for weeks."

What she said made little sense, but Gabe didn't care. He liked seeing her happy and pleased with herself and her secret. He caught both her hands in his, his eyes sweeping from the blaze of her hair to the satin slippers nearly hidden by the full skirted gown. Dressed in clinging satin or coarse denim, or only the lacy shadows of rustling leaves, she was beautiful. He wanted her—to hold and keep her and be with her always.

He loved her! He had almost from the first. Perhaps he'd known it in that part of himself that was the essence of the man he was. But he'd been blinded by the first surge of passion exploding out of nowhere, and like a nova he'd expected it to destroy itself in its own fire. Now he discovered that beneath its brilliance had lain something basic, something stronger for its gentleness. It had flourished, endured, become an irrevocable part of him, needing only this shattering moment of admission to end his doubts. In what seemed another life, he'd come to Stonebridge worn and weary, a stranger to love. And now that he'd found her, now that he'd caught the star? Dear God! He couldn't lose her.

Caroline turned in a whirl of her skirts; she missed his ragged breath. "Come on," she commanded, loosening one hand as she nearly dragged him with her through the kitchen to the service porch. She stopped abruptly, so unexpectedly that only his arms about her kept him from bowling her over.

"Here." She pointed toward a bulky package that boasted a bow the size of a dinner plate.

He shook his head as if to clear it, struggling to deal calmly with his discovery. He fought the need to fold her in his arms, to tell her his feelings and love her. Through a haze he saw her smile falter at what must seem reluctance to accept her gift. At last he forced out, "It's not my birthday."

Caroline's face brightened, she interpreted his hesitation as confusion. "Does it have to be? Can't a gift be for any reason? Why not simply because I'm glad I know you, or even for a welcome home?"

He remembered that once he'd told her as he danced with her in the darkness that he had no home. Now he did. Caroline was home. He knelt before the package. "Do I open it now?"

"Please." She nodded. Gabe saw again her young heart and her joy in simple pleasures.

With a disregard for the outward trappings of a beautiful package, he ripped the paper away. The ribbon went one way, the wrapping another, then he was still. Not even a rustle of the profusion of paper broke his concentration.

"It's beautiful, Caroline." Spread about him, wrought in heavy black metal, were andirons and fire tools and a delicate but sturdy fire screen. He knew they would serve him well. Sitting back on his haunches he looked up at her.

"Do you like them?" she waited, hardly daring to breathe, anxious in her need to please him.

"How could I not?" He answered her question with a question as he looked again at her gift. The screen was most arresting. Oversized, it was wonderfully suitable for the cabin's huge fireplace. A fine mesh stretched tautly across the framework, and at its base, hidden amid long blades of grass and clusters of Queen Anne's lace, fashioned in black iron, was a bold J flanked by a smaller G and a K. With his fingers Gabe traced the exquisite shapes. Caroline's design, produced by Shiloh's forge.

"I wanted something special, but I was afraid..." Doubt was in her voice as it trailed away.

"It's perfect. The cabin itself is special and everything that goes in it should be. This will become an heirloom. My initials and your flower, they go well together."

"Gabriel Kent Jackson. It's a good, strong name."

"I can't remember discussing my full name."

"Shiloh told me."

Gabe stood, clasping her hand in his. "I've known for a long time that I could never see another field of Queen Anne's lace without thinking of you. Now I'll have that reminder always in my home. Thank you."

Caroline lifted his hands to her lips. She kissed each once, and smiled at him. "I hope it serves you well, in a home that brings you happiness."

"It will." He wanted desperately to hold her again, but it was late, and the Harvest Ball and Pete waited. "We should be going," he reminded her in a husky voice.

"You're right. Just let me catch Joe. I could leave him out of his cage, but I'd rather not." She spoke as she led him back to the den.

"Where is he?" Gabe scanned the room, but the parrot was nowhere to be seen.

"He's hiding. It's a game he loves," she said.

"Then why don't we leave him?" Gabe suggested. "You said he can stay out of his cage."

"I suppose you're right," Caroline agreed.

She gathered up her shawl and followed him to the door. As he opened it for her she hesitated. Her eyes were wide. "Gabe! What if he's changed?" she whispered. Her hands were hidden in the folds of her dress, but he knew they were clenched against the sudden surge of nervous dread.

"Pete hasn't changed, Caroline," he assured her. "Not in the things that matter. He'll be as handsome as his father in his uniform, and you'll be proud. I promise."

The home of the chancellor of Stonebridge Academy was the site of the Harvest Ball. Tonight would mark the end of the quarantine that all school newcomers had to observe. Eager families, and in some cases, sweethearts, milled about its grounds.

An uneven brick walk wound through a garden still resplendent with late-blooming flowers. Baskets of ferns hung from low limbs and huge urns filled to overflowing with yellow chrysanthemums flanked the stairs that led to the house.

It was through this garden and up these steps that the elders, or seniors, would march with their partners beneath the drawn sabres of underclassmen. It had always been a moving sight, but tonight would be special.

"Will you see Pete before the ball begins?" Gabe laid his hand over Caroline's as it rested in the crook of his arm.

"Not allowed," she told him as she searched the crowd for a stolen look nevertheless. Suddenly her fingers dug into him. "There! There they are."

Shoulder to shoulder, with stern martial grace, the cadets marched to a silent cadence. In parade dress of slate-blue jackets that topped snow-white trousers, they moved as a unit, their black-booted heels striking the bricks firmly and their faces calm beneath the brim of their plumed black hats. One by one, with a precision turn, they took their places lining the walk.

"I see him," Caroline whispered into Gabe's shoulder. Tears of pride were stinging. "He's beautiful."

"That must be how she looked when she first danced with Mark," Shiloh murmured to Scotty and Gabe as they stood side by side on the fringes of the crowd.

"She's lovely." Gabe's gaze followed her, mesmerized.

"Aye, she's quite a lass, and the boy'll be every inch the man his father was." Scotty's burr had thickened as a suspicious brilliance shone in his eyes.

None looked away from the tiny figure who danced so proudly in the arms of her tall son.

Caroline smiled and Pete laughed. And the flush of her cheeks told all who saw that she'd never been happier in her life. Pete, newly mature as he'd become steeped in the traditions of the academy, held her comfortably, much of his adolescent awkwardness forgotten. As he looked down at her, his face glowed.

The room was filled with women. Some attractive, some not. Some solemn, some gay. But none was as special or as beautiful as his mother.

Julie whirled by, held circumspectly at arm's length by her husband. She spoke quickly in passing to Caroline and Pete, then flashed a look of triumph at Gabe and Shiloh.

"She made it," Gabe chuckled.

"Just barely," Shiloh commented in a low voice. "Kevin said her contractions started an hour ago."

"What!" Gabe caught himself and lowered his voice to a less noticeable level. "And she's here?"

"She did a number on Kevin, insisted that it would pass the time."

"But good grief, Shiloh! Contractions!"

"I know," he agreed, disquieted. "But she assures Kevin it will be hours yet. Something about first babies taking their own sweet time."

The music changed tempo. Hiram huffed by with his plump little wife. Riley and Butch danced with pretty blondes who were clearly twins. Georgie Lee swooped by with a sultry brunette in his arms.

Beyond the gyrating bodies the watching men saw Julie stop. Her body shuddered, her hand going instinctively to the swell of her abdomen. She spoke to her startled husband and his marked pallor was like a beacon. His arm went about her as he led her through the crowd. Julie had time for only one quick look as he fussed worriedly over her. With a gleeful grin spreading over her face, she waggled her fingers at Shiloh.

"Excuse me." Waiting for no reply, Shiloh strode away and was soon lost among the dancers. Once, as they parted, Gabe saw his dark head bent over Julie's, his hand resting on Kevin's arm. Then they were blocked from view by Hiram and his wife.

Perfume wafted about him, and Gabe longed for Caroline.

"Begorrah! The woman had drenched herself in toilet water." Scotty crinkled his nose in distaste.

"Gentlemen." Shiloh was back. "If all goes as it should, we'll have babies before the night's out."

"Should we tell Caroline?" Gabe asked as the three of them turned to find her among the dancers.

"She'd only worry and insist that she should go to be with Julie. Look at her," Shiloh said. "She's looked forward to this day since Pete entered the academy. Let's not spoil it for her."

"She's sure to miss Julie."

"She will that," Scotty agreed with Gabe. "Best tell her the truth, or at least a portion of it."

"She promised me a dance. I'll go claim it now. Maybe she'll believe that Julie was tired and left early.

She'll be as mad as Hades later." Shiloh grinned. "But I trust the two of you to protect me."

"We can try," Gabe said doubtfully, remembering the scorching he'd gotten the last time Caroline lost her temper.

"After our dance, I think I'll run over to the hospital. Kevin might need some company. Time now to beard the tigress; wish me luck." The last was tossed back at them as Shiloh threaded his way into the crowd.

"He's a brave lad," Scotty said. "At least this time we won't have a landslide."

"We hope."

The night air had grown cool. Shawls had appeared as the ladies joined their men on the veranda. Music and light spilled through the windows and the open doorway as Gabe and Pete strolled through the garden.

"How's the academy?" he asked the boy. Gabe had taken this opportunity to steal a moment alone with Pete while Caroline danced first with Shiloh, then Scotty, and next with members of her crew.

"Fine, sir."

"Are you enjoying the regimented atmosphere?"

"Yes, sir."

"Will you make the military your career?"

"I don't think so, sir. But for a while it will be okay. In a way I feel as if I really know my dad, now. For the first time I'm doing the things he did, walking where he walked." Pete's voice trailed away. He was too young, too inexperienced to find the words, but it didn't matter, Gabe understood.

"Will you follow in his footsteps in college? Do you think premed is what you'd like to do?"

"Maybe. I haven't decided yet. Stonebridge has meant a lot to me because of my father, but if I choose medicine, it will be because it's what I want to do. Mom will understand; I believe Dad would, too."

Brava, Caroline! You've done it. You've created a legacy...and a man. Gab thought he would burst with pride. He wanted to shout it and laugh at the same time. Instead he calmed himself, settling for a change of subject. "Any time for tennis?" He hadn't known the boy well, but they liked each other and shared this interest. "Going to make the team?"

"Oh, wow! I mean..." Pete forgot his new dignity.

"'Oh, wow' will be fine." Gabe laughed. "How's the new serve?"

"Terrific. I did it just like you told me. It puts a top spin on the ball not too many of the new guys can handle. Just as soon as I get leave, I'm going to let Beth have it, right in the chops!"

Gabe grinned again into the darkness. That was still Caroline's Pete inside the starched correctness of the uniform. "Don't be too rough on her. She's still a kid."

"She's a knock-kneed, wall-eyed monster."

"I think I'll ask you to repeat that in about a year."

"I won't change my mind."

"We'll see." Gabe stopped at a long row of hedge. As he lounged against a tall post topped by a bell, he broached the subject that had tormented him for hours. "Your mother's been alone for a long time."

"Yes, sir. I really worried that she'd be lonesome when I was gone."

"She misses you. But she wants more than anything for you to follow in your father's footsteps if it's really what you want."

"I wanted it bad. But—"

"How would you feel if she married again?"

Pete's face lit up. "Man, that'd be great! When did Shiloh ask her? Did she say yes?"

"Shiloh isn't going to ask her, Pete. I am."

"Oh." Gabe watched the guileless young face run the gamut from surprise to disappointment, from consideration to acceptance. "Hey, that'd be all right. I don't know you so well yet, but it should be okay."

"I take it I have your approval?"

"Yes, sir. As long as you have Mom's too."

Gabe laughed tightly, attracting the curious interest of a couple who strolled nearby. In his youthful candor Pete had gone straight to the heart of the matter.

"She's going away on a business trip tomorrow. Will you pop the question before then?" The boy forgot his newfound dignity in his eagerness.

"I hope to tonight. But, Pete—" Gabe spoke with an unintended harshness as he faced a thought too painful to conceive "—she might say no."

"Yes, sir." There was sympathy in the young voice. "I know."

Nine

"Tired?" Gabe asked. Caroline had been unusually quiet since Pete had wished them good-night and excused himself at curfew.

"Not a bit." She looked up at the star-studded sky that spread like a canopy over the garden. "I'm too happy to be tired."

"Happy about Pete?"

"Yes." The single word was filled with a new and deeper contentment.

"You saw tonight that he'll be the man his father never had the chance to be."

"The confirmation of all Mark's dreams. He had so little time to dream, and none to make them come true." She grew quiet, her face reflecting the tragedy of a laughing young dreamer whose life had been destroyed and with it very nearly her own. Determinedly she refused to let sorrow rule her. When she spoke again her voice was soft, but filled with strength. "Are dreams really lost as long as someone is left who can fulfill them?"

"His son."

An acknowledgement was unnecessary; Caroline knew it as well as Gabe. "Pete has his father's courage, his sense of honor, and there's a touch of his laughter in that crooked little half smile. Mark's legacy will see him through the future. I know that now." She turned her face to the sky again. "I've never seen the stars so bright."

Gabe murmured a thoughtful agreement but he had no time for stars. Written on Caroline's face was the openness he'd been waiting for. She'd come to the end of a long road with a solitary goal. A pledge she'd made to herself had been accomplished. She'd done it willingly, with a loyal heart.

Tonight she'd discharged a trust of love, and with it had said a gentle goodbye to Mark. Gabe first understood it when she had looked at Pete with the shine of pride in her face and seen that he was, indeed, beautiful. Perhaps even Caroline didn't realize it yet, but she'd come to a new beginning.

Gabe stepped closer and their bodies nearly touched as he bent to her. Caroline lifted her head, and eyes that had always held the serenity of acceptance were grave as they looked back at him. Then her lips softened in a smile that was sweet without the bitter. The restraint that had guided him for countless weeks snapped, his armor of lighthearted banter crumbled. He drew his arms about her and crushed her to him.

He couldn't be gentle. The hunger that lived within him wouldn't allow it. The desire that had been his constant companion since he'd held her in his arms,

sooty and wet and incredibly beautiful, demanded a
reckoning. His searching kiss, his caressing tongue,
sought to claim again the fire of her passion. It had
slumbered there in her heart, waiting, a part of her
that none since Mark had touched. None but he, Gabe
Jackson, the wanderer who had come home.

As Caroline moved to meet his kiss, her hands
trailed up his arms, over his shoulders and throat, to
touch the mass of his hair. It was like satin as she cradled his head in her palms. Her wrist lay at the hollow
beneath his ear. The beat of her own pulse blended
with his and she was as hungry as he. Her lips parted,
she accepted and met his urgency.

They were driven by a common need to touch and
be touched, to hold and be held. Each kiss led to another, and each caress to still another. Each reaching
deeper, coming ever nearer to that elusive core that
held and protected the treasured gift of self.

Gabe's hands circled her waist, moving with a
slowness that agonized to cup the fullness of her
breasts. The satin of her gown might have been flesh
for it served as no barrier. A soft purr of pleasure
sounded deep in his chest as nipples grew taut and
hard in response. Caroline made no answering sound
but surged against him, seeking more, offering more.

Shrubs rustled and a stone rattled nearby, reminding that others strolled the garden. As she stepped
away he let her go with a low, frustrated groan. His
hands were reluctant as they readjusted the neckline of
her gown, lingering against the dusky swell only half
hidden by the discreet ruffling of lace. Some small cry
she made drew his attention to her face. The beginning of a smile curved his mouth as he touched her
throat.

He kissed her once more, lightly, gravely. It was the kiss of ritual, the seal of a binding promise. "My Caroline," he whispered hoarsely.

Her name. Only her name. Said many times in many ways, but on his lips it had become the brand of possession.

Possession! The word seared her brain, it served as a warning. Common sense and reason reared their heads as Caroline realized she was poised on the brink of... what? She had come a long way, learned a great deal, and found a fledgling courage. But was she brave enough to face what lay ahead with Gabe? Was she strong enough? Doubt was the single dark current in the bright flowing river of her new happiness. In moments of lonely quiet the question haunted her. She would never again retreat from the world. Gabe had made that impossible. But was she ready for the risks of loving such a man? The answer lay in herself. It would be the key to the rest of her life.

Laughter and conversation drifted on the evening breeze, encircling them, growing nearer. For the first time Caroline and Gabe were aware that the music had stopped and dancers filled the garden as they took advantage of the break to walk in the moonlight. Couples moved one after another from the veranda to the garden and back again; it was only a matter of time before some eager young lovers would stumble onto their secluded corner.

Gabe's smile grew strained. "I've become a master at the art of bad timing."

"Perhaps this once it's for the best." Caroline took his arm. "The dance is nearly over. Both Shiloh and Scotty seemed to have disappeared after Julie and

Kevin left. I've danced even more than I care to, why don't we go home?''

Caroline put her key stealthily into the front door lock. Like conspirators she and Gabe crept through the darkened foyer.

"Joe's been restless lately. We'd better go carefully, unless you want to wake him."

"God forbid," Gabe grumbled. "Not any night, but especially not tonight."

At the doorway to the den she paused. "Can you find your way from here. I'd like to freshen up."

"Don't be long." He touched her shoulder, his fingers lingering. "We need to talk."

"I know."

Gabe waited until she'd gone, with only her fragrance lingering about him, before he moved blindly into the den. A sudden sharp tug at his ankle nearly tripped him. He thought at first he'd bumped into something. Then he felt it again, holding, pulling. Instinctively he jerked away to free himself.

Geronimo!

The scream rocked the room. With a whirr of wings and a flashing beak a tiny body threw itself against his ankles. He was attacked by a streak of red and yellow that danced and darted, beating against him. Joe! Gabe knew there was no real danger, but he dared not move. One misstep and he might cause the abominable creature lasting injury. Out of desperation he bent, snatched at the bird, caught a handful of tail feathers and held fast. But his toe hooked the corner of a low table and sent him sprawling.

"Caroline!"

Geronimo!

The shriek so close to his ear was nearly deafening, but Gabe refused to let go, and he still couldn't move. A vase filled with fresh flowers had tumbled from the table and spilled onto his back. His hands were occupied with the struggling bird. Caroline was his only help.

"Caroline!" he bellowed in desperation.

Running footsteps stopped at the door, the room was flooded with light. Caroline stood by the switch blinking against the brightness, then concentrated all her energies toward holding back her laughter. How could they have forgotten that Joe had not been in his cage?

"You called?"

"Twice," Gabe answered tersely, still refusing to relinquish his hostage.

"Was there something you needed?"

"No, of course not. I always lie on the floor with a scraggly parrot in my hands and a flower pot on my foot."

She stepped closer. "Which would you like for me to take first—Joe, the vase, or the flowers?"

"The vase. I'm not letting this menace free for a second. I'm personally going to see that he spends the rest of this night in his cage."

Her shoulders were shaking as she knelt to pick up the flowers and vase. "Would you like for me to remove the flowers, or would you rather wear them?"

"Caroline." She didn't look at him—she didn't dare—but she knew from his tone that he was glowering.

One by one, she slowly picked the scattered flowers from around him and returned them to the vase. "There now, good as new. Or almost."

"Thanks." Joe flapped his wings violently and Gabe almost lost his hold. "Bird, you're going to be sporting a crew cut for a tail if you don't behave. You've had your revenge, better make the most of it."

"Revenge?" Caroline asked.

"I'd threatened him once."

"But surely you don't think—"

"That he understood?" Gabe said grimly. "Of course I do."

With a smug growl and a smoothing of his ruffled feathers, Joe grew quiet. Still holding him by neck and feet, and ignoring the fact that Caroline seemed suddenly to be choking with laughter, Gabe struggled to his feet and marched in squishing shoes to the cage. He not ungently set the bird on his perch and shut the door with meticulous care. He turned, hands on hips, to face her.

"You can laugh now," he said solemnly, then burst into laughter of his own.

Much later, when there was order out of chaos, he kissed the tears of laughter from her face and pulled her from the sofa. "It's late. Walk me to the door and kiss me good-night and I'll be on my way. You'll be leaving for New Orleans in the morning and you should get some rest. We'll have that talk when you get back."

"All right," she agreed.

Gabe didn't miss the look of relief that crossed her face. Tonight had been filled with change and she needed time to sort out her thoughts. In his haste he had meant to settle matters between them as quickly as possible. But in retrospect, he could see that it was too soon, he'd very nearly made a mistake. Grudgingly he admitted that he was indebted to Joe.

"Joe." The bird stopped its grooming, the black eyes fastened on Gabe. "There might be hope for us yet."

"Are you declaring a truce?" Caroline asked.

"I think I have to." Gabe turned away from the cage. "Now, are you sure you don't want me to take you to the airport in the morning?"

"I'm sure. I need some time, Gabe. There are questions chasing questions around in my mind. I'll be gone a week and I want to use the time to get completely away, to regain some perspective and to know my own mind."

"Then you won't call me?"

"No."

"And you don't want me to call you."

"I'd rather you didn't."

"I'll respect your wishes, but I'll miss you."

"I'll miss you."

"I'll hold on to that." Gabe kissed her lightly. He dared not take her in his arms. If he did, he knew he would never leave, and right or wrong, she wouldn't make him. "Good night, love. Good night, Joe."

A satisfied chuckle rumbled from Joe's dark corner.

The morning sky was gray when Caroline turned her small car into the inn's service entrance. Careful to make no noise, she pushed the door closed but didn't shut it. Like a thief she raced across the graveled lot of the delivery dock and up the outside stairs that led to the bedroom of Shiloh's apartment. Out of breath from the climb she lifted her hand to knock, hesitated, bit her lip, then rapped firmly. It seemed an eternity before the door opened and Shiloh stood before her.

"Caroline!" A look of alarm crossed his face as he looped the belt of his robe loosely about his waist. "Is anything wrong?" He took her hand in his and led her inside. "Is it Pete?"

"No." Caroline caught her breath with an effort. "I didn't mean to alarm you. Nothing's wrong."

"Are you sure?" His palm at her forehead told him she was well. A quick, appraising look at her body assured him that she was as unharmed as she was healthy. In a second look at her eyes he saw dark circles. He laced her fingers through his as he sat her down on the bed. "You don't look as if you slept last night."

"I didn't. At least not until almost dawn. Then I overslept. That's why I'm in a rush. I meant to ask last night but you disappeared before I could. Will you see to Joe while I'm gone, and the house, and if Pete should need . . ."

"I'll take care of it. But what about you?"

"I'm fine, Shiloh. Honestly, it's just that it was a long night."

"Is it Gabe?"

Her shoulders slumped, she couldn't lie to him. "Yes."

"Are you in love with him?"

"I think so," she said softly. Then with a slow shake of her head she said, "No, that's not quite right. I don't think. I know."

"Then what's the problem?"

"Me. I'm the problem."

"Can I help?"

"No, dear friend." She tightened her fingers about those that clasped them. "This I face alone."

"Will you see him before you go?"

"No. We said goodbye last night." She stood and stepped toward the door. With a thoughtful look on her face she turned back to him. "Shiloh?" She frowned as he rose to stand before her. "Have you ever wondered why we never fell in love?"

"It just wasn't in the cards." He shrugged. "We were too comfortable together, and love isn't that. At least not for a long, long time. We were destined to be friends, the best of friends."

"But you do have somebody? Somebody who isn't . . . comfortable."

"I have my moments, in certain circles." He chuckled.

Caroline flushed. In the years of their friendship she'd never pried into his most private life. She pressed a palm against a heated cheek. "I shall go. I'll have to dash to catch my plane as it is. And you can get on with your day."

"Actually, I was just going to bed. Alone, I assure you." He grinned and Caroline laughed. "I was at the hospital all night. Julie had her twins. A boy and a girl."

"One of each! How wonderful! I wish I could see them," she said wistfully.

"But you can't, and they understand. All of them, including Kevin, are fine. Julie sends her love and says have a safe journey."

"Tell her I'll call her from New Orleans." She checked her watch, then kissed his cheek. "Gotta run."

She was almost out the door when she stopped and turned. "The women in those circles you were speaking of. Any of them would be lucky to have you for a lover. You're quite a man. You can tell them that for me. And, Shiloh?"

"Yes?"

"You're more than my dearest friend."

Shiloh nodded gravely. "I'm the brother you never had. Now scoot. Have a safe flight and I'll see you in a week."

New Orleans. A beautiful city—of courtyards and balconies, a place of excitement and contrasts. But not for Caroline. She strolled the Vieux Carré, the French Quarter, and found it lacking. As she sat under the portico at Café du Monde drinking the traditional cup of café au lait and discussing the plans for a new home with her clients, she found herself inexplicably at a loss for words. Listening to original jazz in Preservation Hall left her somber, dull and angry at herself for it. She'd done these things before and loved them. Anticipation of their remembered pleasure had been an enticement for this journey.

The Williamsons, clients and friends, first of the father and then of the daughter, had done their very best to entertain her. To her credit, Caroline tried. She put on a happy face that fooled no one. Although her designs and her drawings were good, they were missing the flair that made her work unique. No one knew it better than she. One crumpled drawing followed another into the trash, until Margaret Williamson took matters into her own kind hands.

"Go home, Caroline. You're miserable here."

"But your house," she protested.

"It can wait. We've had that land and the dream of this special house for years. A few more months won't matter. Go home. Come to terms with what's bothering you."

"I'll think about it."

"You do that." Margaret's wrinkled, beringed hand patted her arm gently as she wished her good-night.

In the privacy of her room, Caroline paced. Once, twice, three times she circled it. Each time she hesitated beside the telephone. The third time she succumbed. With the receiver tucked at her chin, she dialed the number and waited for an answer. A small ache was just beginning when a voice heavy with sleep cut short the seventh ring.

"Hello. Hello. Who's there? Caroline? Is that you?"

Carefully, not trusting herself to speak, she returned the receiver to its cradle. She'd broken her own rule, but she wasn't sorry. Her decision was made, she was going home.

Suddenly a mind grown stale was brimming with ideas that fairly flew from pen to paper. She worked through the night and into the afternoon of the following day, barely leaving herself enough time to catch an evening flight. But the ideas were good. She knew it, the Williamsons knew it. After promising she would return soon, she boarded the late flight that would take her home with their blessing.

There was a prophecy of winter in the chill of the night as Caroline raced her small car over twists and turns of the narrow road. The beam of her headlights flashed erratically over field and fence and stream. Fallen leaves scattered under skidding tires as she touched her brake for the last turn. Then the inn was before her.

She stopped before the main entrance, spared a minute for a quick glance in the mirror, snatched the keys from the ignition and climbed from the car.

The lobby was deserted as she crossed it. Her footsteps thudded softly as she rushed up the stairs. Gabe's room was on the second floor, third door on the right. Before it she paused, raked her hand nervously through her cap of curls, then rapped with false courage.

It had been four days. What if absence didn't make the heart grow fonder? What if time and distance between them had shown him that he didn't want her after all? What if...

"Nitwit!" she scolded. "Gabe knows his own mind. A few days won't change it."

She knocked again.

"Hiya, Caroline." Tim, dressed in his uniform, carried a room-service tray. "Looking for Mr. Jackson? He checked out early this morning."

"What?" She was so taken by surprise that his words refused to register in her tired brain.

"Mr. Jackson checked out," Tim repeated, unaware that Caroline's world had just spun out of control.

"Checked out? Where did he go?" She looked at him with an empty expression and knew the question was useless. He wouldn't know. She slumped against the wall as fatigue from sleepless nights and long hours at the drawing board caught up with her. She tried to force her numb mind to think, but it refused.

"Caroline." She lifted her head slowly. Shiloh stood at the end of the long corridor. "He moved to the cabin. He meant it to be a surprise. Go to him. He'll be there."

"I'm home early," she said inanely.

"It doesn't matter. He'll be waiting. Go to him, tell him you love him. Build a life with him, give him strong sons and beautiful daughters."

Relief flooded over her, but something in Shiloh's tone caught at her. "And what about you?" she asked softly, gently. "Will there be sons and daughters for you?"

"No, Caroline. Not for me, not ever." The massive shoulders seemed to bow a bit. Perhaps it was a trick of the light, but in the dimness his eyes seemed to flash with a strange glitter.

"Shiloh." She reached out to him, suddenly understanding the full meaning of his words.

"It's over and done with, an irrevocable part of the past. You mustn't concern yourself with it—not when the future is yours for the making. Go to him, Caroline. Don't waste a precious moment."

She nodded, unable to speak, remembering the ashen-faced man who had held concern for Julie's unborn children, the dark satyr who had instructed a herd of children with infinite patience, the stranger who had become friend and confidant to her own son. Despite the ache in her throat she smiled at him and whispered, "I'm glad you were Mark's friend... and mine. I love you, Shiloh."

"I know," he said quietly. "Now go."

Smoke rose from the cabin's chimney and a faint light shone through its windows. For the second time in the hour Caroline rapped at a door that she hoped would lead to Gabe. For the second time, there was no answer. She tested the lock, the knob turned. The door opened, and she stepped inside.

A fire burned behind the screen that had been her gift. There was no other light as the flame cast dancing shadows over the room. Ezra's handmade furniture, repaired and polished, gleamed with a low luster. An afghan and gaily printed pillows were strewn over the sofa. On a stand in the corner, Joe slept with his head tucked into a wing. The drone of the shower was accompanied by an off-key whistling of some indeterminate tune.

Gabe. Caroline extended her hands toward the warmth of the fire and smiled, and waited.

Her wait wasn't long. The water stopped, leaving only the sound of the crackling fire and the pounding of her heart. Then he was there, framed in the doorway. His body was bare except for the towel wrapped and tucked at his waist. His torso glistened in the flickering light, the muscles of his chest and shoulders were deep and rippled with each move. Droplets of water lay against his hair. He was the most magnificent man she'd ever known.

His eyes found hers and something stirred in them. His chest rose sharply in one short breath, then he was utterly still. Caroline's mouth grew dry. Her muscles tightened against the sensation deep in the pit of her stomach as desire stirred, awakened. She wanted to speak but couldn't.

"You're home early. Why, Caroline?"

"Because there's something I have to tell you." She took a step toward him and the words she ached to say tumbled out. "I love you. I have for a long while, and for as little or as long as I'm allowed to have you, I need you. You can wander the world if you must, so long as you come home to me, then I'll cherish every second of every minute of every day. Without you I'll never be complete, but I know now that if ever I must lose you, I'll survive. If I can just have this time.''

His frozen remoteness dissolved. In two strides he was before her, so close she felt the ragged rush of his breath. He searched her face, her eyes, finding truth. Then the need, the desire he'd held in check, spiraled to new heights.

''Oh, love, come here.'' He pulled her to him. His hands cupped the back of her head as he drew her lips to his. His kisses were urgent beneath the tenderness as he murmured words of his love. His caressing exploration led to her throat and to the buttons of her simple dress. With exquisite purpose his hands roamed her body until the last of her clothing lay in a pool about her feet.

''Dear Lord!'' he whispered as he stepped away. ''You're even more beautiful than I remembered.''

Caroline waited, wondrously sure, feeling only the exultion of one who loved and was loved. Gabe stroked her breast and she trembled.

''Touch me, Caroline. I like for you to touch me.''

Caroline obeyed. She touched him with her gaze, then with her hands. Tentatively she brushed them across his hair, then buried her fingers in its darkness. Then restlessly untangling from the still-damp strands, her fingers strayed over his face, his lips, then stroked fleetingly over his chest. As her confidence grew, so did her desire. She reveled in the feel of his strength, in the smoothness of his skin. She felt an urgent need for more as her hands fell to the towel that was his only covering. In an instant it slithered to join her own clothing on the floor. Her hands at his hips brought him hard against her. A low groan of sweetest agony rumbled through him.

Swiftly he caught her up in his arms. Her slight weight was nothing as he climbed the steps to the sleeping loft. In that tiny alcove, he laid her on the bed that had been readied for the night. He stood over her, captivated by the invitation he saw. "Say my name," he pleaded. "Say it as you did the first day."

"Gabe." It was a whisper filled with a waiting love.

"On your lips it becomes an endearment."

"It is. I think it always was." She caught his hand in hers. "Make love to me, Gabe. Love me as you did in the meadow."

He came down to her, easing his body over hers, waiting as she grew familiar with the weight of him. His wandering caresses were warm and strong as they touched and claimed each new part of her. When he felt the wildness of her need for him, he drew back. He looked at her and she felt the blue gaze reaching to the gift she waited to give. Her self, her heart, all that she would ever be.

"Caroline," he murmured. "So brave, so strong."

"Not so brave nor so strong—at least not where you were concerned." She moved her fingers over his chest to the hard muscles of his shoulders. "Never where you were concerned," she whispered.

He leaned over her, looking intently into her face. "Why did you leave me in the meadow?"

"I was afraid."

Gabe drew a sharp breath. At last she'd said it. From the first he'd watched her grow and bloom, gaining strength, reentering the world. But not once had she put a name to the malady that had nearly crippled her. She'd faced it and battled it in silence but kept it in the darkness. Now, very calmly, as if it were the most natural thing in the world, she spoke of it, offering to him even that part of herself. He felt a gathering of tears at the sound of her sweet whispering.

"Mark and I were like children, laughing and loving, and when he was gone I thought there could be no more. Then you arrived. You touched me, and there was fire that ripped through me, leaving no part unscathed. In some deep, dark place there was something hot and wild, wanting to be free. It threatened to consume me, and yet it was beautiful." She stroked the side of his face. "So beautiful that I was afraid. Afraid to love you. Afraid it couldn't last."

Gabe closed his eyes, a shudder passed through him. "Don't you know that I've been afraid, too? From the first moment I saw you, I've been afraid to trust what I felt. Afraid to believe I could love so."

"Not anymore," she whispered. "Not anymore."

"Not anymore. Someday," he murmured against her lips, "I'll tell you about a falling star and the gift it brought me." Then he was kissing her, taking her with him into that rare magic only they could share. Gently he took her, accepting her gift even as he gave his own. At the first virile possession, some long-ago memory of a young girl caught in the wonders of first love danced fleetingly in her mind and was forgotten. She arched against him, reveling in the very wildness he unleashed, rejoicing in the passions of a mature woman.

Caroline lay in Gabe's arms with tears on her cheeks. She cried in her joy in this man by her side. Gabe, who had battered her defenses, then awakened her to a love that surpassed fear. He'd helped to set her free of a life lived only in memory; then with gentle caresses and tender kisses had made her captive again—a captive bound by the power of love. Soon he would be gone, but he'd return to her, time and again. It would be enough.

"Tears?" Gabe's thumb was incredibly light as he stroked the wetness from her face.

"Happy tears." She evaded the question in his words and snuggled into his shoulder.

"It's more than that, Caroline." He rolled over until her body lay beneath his. "Don't put secrets between us. Tell me."

"I'm just borrowing trouble." Her effort at a smile missed the mark. "You'll be leaving soon. I've always known you would, but I'm missing you already."

"I'm not going anywhere."

"But your job!"

"There are others. I thought perhaps there might even be a spot for me at Douglas Construction." He grinned at her blank look. "I can assure you I bring a measure of expertise to the job. I even have references."

"It wouldn't work." Caroline frowned, and struggled to rise. Sensing her agitation, Gabe let her go. Absently she picked up a shirt he'd thrown aside and shrugged into it.

He hid a smile as the cuffs fell inches below the tips of her fingers, and the tail to midthigh, revealing a fetching length of shapely leg. It made concentration difficult, but Gabe knew he must. He folded his arms and began to wage his debate. "Suppose you tell me why it won't work."

Caroline whirled in her pacing to face him, unconscious that the supple material of the shirt revealed more than it concealed. "It won't work. It can't. You're not accustomed to the quiet life of a small town. Before long you'll be bored here and you'll want to leave. You'll have to leave."

"I see. You're basing all this logic on your theory that I'll be bored here. You must not think much of me, Caroline."

"No! It isn't that at all. I'm trying to face facts. You love me, and I love you. I love you enough to let you go, so long as you keep coming back to me for a little while. I know that a sleepy town like Stonebridge is deadly dull after the real world."

His roar of laughter startled her. "'Dull.'" he gasped. "'Dull.' she says. Sweet heaven! The world itself is dull by comparison to what I've found in Stonebridge. Where else would I encounter the captivating joys of chimney fires and a fireman with a sooty smile so lovely it's heartbreaking? Where but in Stonebridge would I find the heady mixture of landslides and bulldozers, dandelion wine and an attack parrot, or a blue-eyed renegade that I think is going to be the best friend I ever had? Where else could I find a boy who's the very image of a man I wish I'd known and is all I could want in a son? But most of all, where else under the shining sun would I find a woman who brings excitement to every day and makes life worth living? Don't you know that the real world, as you call it, offers me nothing after what I've found here."

"But—"

"But, nothing. I've asked you for a job and whether or not I get it, I'm staying. At any rate, I don't believe in marriages with long-term separations built into them.''

''Is that a proposal?'' Caroline's eyes were huge.

''It's not as romantic as I intended, but I think it's obvious. I have Pete's permission and his approval. So, what's it to be? Do I have to tell him you turned me down?''

''No. I mean, yes.'' She took a deep breath and started again. ''Yes, you can have the job. You can have the whole damn company. No, you don't have to tell Pete I turned you down, because yes, I'll marry you. Just as soon as you want me.''

''How about yesterday.'' Gabe opened his arms and Caroline flew into them. As her body folded into his he whispered against her lips, ''Don't you know, love, that I could never leave you.''

Ten

___

Gabe lifted his lips slowly from Caroline's. His eyes feasted on her upturned face. In their year together he'd never tired of kissing her awake, waiting after each kiss for her dark lashes to sweep upward as her eyes opened. It was always there, that sleepy look of satisfaction. Yet each time it was new, each time the love he saw there was as fresh as the first time.

"Good morning," he murmured as the delightful gaze focused on him.

"Good morning." Caroline stretched and smiled up at him. "I'm turning into a lazybones in my old age. You didn't bargain for that, did you?"

"I bargained for whatever it took to get you. It was a bargain well made. I've no regrets." With a gentle touch he coiled a curl, worn longer now, about his finger. "Not even for landslides and bulldozers, or even the bird. It's all a part of loving you. I wouldn't have missed it for the world.''

Caroline made a soft, contented sound, her hands slid over the sleek hardness of his body. Playfully she nuzzled his cheek with her nose. ''Mmm, you smell good.'' *Quiet evenings, good books, old velvet and jeans…and love hidden in every look.* He was all those things and more. ''Have you already had your shower?''

''Hours ago. In fact our son and I have already had breakfast. Toast and coffee for me, a bottle for him, then we took our morning stroll down by the new lake. We discussed how good the fishing's going to be when he and the fish get a little older.''

''And what sage comment did he have about that?'' Caroline sighed as Gabe slipped into bed beside her. His hand curled naturally about the fullness of her breast.

''I'm afraid his conversation consisted mostly of grunts, and I could have sworn I heard a giggle, and of course a yawn or two.''

''Do you think he needs a nap before the christening?'' Caroline turned on her side and snuggled closer against the bareness of his chest.

''All taken care of. He's bathed and powdered and changed. When I left them, Joe was singing a lullaby, and he was sleeping on his knees with his bottom in the air. It looked distinctly uncomfortable, but who am I to say?''

''His father, that's who.'' Gabe's hands were busy at the lacy tie of her gown, and Caroline shivered as his cool hands stroked her warm flesh, stealing her breath from her. ''I think he knows already how lucky he is to have a father like you.''

"I thought we were the lucky ones." There was a husky note of loving in his voice.

"We are. When we first saw him in the nursery among all the other babies, an angry papoose with his shock of black hair and his dark skin, it was so easy to see he was ours. But when he turned those fierce blue eyes on you and fastened his hand in your hair and wouldn't let go, I knew you were his. His special person in all the world." She traced the line of Gabe's jaw with her lips. There was a look as fierce as their son's in her own eyes. "He loves you. You're the center of his universe. Will you ever be sorry that he came so soon? Do you ever regret that in our madness we forgot even the most basic precautions?"

"He's a part of our loving, the child of my heart. What could be better than that?" He kissed her slowly, with a curious sense of waiting passion. There was more she had to say. His wandering hand grew still.

"Do we keep you here, this child of your heart and I? After years of traveling the far-flung places of the world, is home and family truly what you want? Loving can be wrong for some. They can be smothered by the very ones they love."

Gabe loomed over her. "You asked me that once before, and I answered. Did you doubt me then? Do you doubt me now? Look at me, Caroline. What do you see?"

There was the hard gleam of hurt deep in him as he waited for her response. Caroline saw his vulnerable need for trust, and the last lingering doubt was shredded from her. She would never ask again. She would never have cause.

Her hands touched his cheeks, gray eyes stared unflinchingly into blue. Her voice was as soft as a baby's smile. "I see Gabe, the love I spent fourteen years of my life waiting for. I see Gabe who loves me, and fills my every need."

His smile was back, tender and unsteady.

"Speaking of need, you don't need this, do you?" Caroline slipped his robe from his shoulders. Her caress was trust and love.

"Caroline?"

"Hmm?"

"Loving you is my freedom." His passion was no longer waiting. It was wild. It was free. It was for Caroline alone.

The weight on his chest woke him. Lazily he opened his eyes and found himself nose to nose with Caroline. Her chin was propped on her folded hands and she watched him solemnly.

"You're awake."

"I am?" he replied sleepily.

"I've been thinking."

"What about?"

"Shiloh, of course."

"Of course, Shiloh." Gabe wrapped his arms about her, breathed deeply of her scent, and brought her head down to rest over his heart. "Tell me what you've been thinking about Shiloh."

"Well, actually, I've been wondering what he's going to think of the baby."

"He knows about the baby. He and Pete and Scotty are the triumvirate of godfathers. It's nearly killed him that he's been out of the country for so long. He'll be here for the christening, and he'll be the second proudest man there. No," Gabe corrected himself, "Pete will be second. But Shiloh will be proud, you can count on it," Gabe assured her indulgently. Caroline worried about Shiloh; she always would. He understood.

"He doesn't know about his name. Maybe we shouldn't have kept it a secret for the christening. Because of... of the prison camp, he'll never have children of his own, but maybe we should have asked permission."

"Permission!" Gabe shook his head and chuckled. "Why on earth should we? As handsome and as intelligent as young Shiloh Mark Jackson is, the man should be flattered to lend us his name."

"Are you sure you hadn't rather give him your name? Gabriel Kent Jackson is a very nice name."

"One in the family's enough."

"Maybe next time," Caroline suggested, then she grinned.

"A funny thought?"

"I was just wondering if anyone ever called you Angel."

"Nobody in his right mind."

"That's what I thought."

"How about a girl next time?" Gabe considered. "One with red hair and huge gray eyes. We could call *her* Angel."

"An angel to help us with those four grandchildren you've decided on."

Gabe tightened his embrace. "You remember!"

"Of course I remember. How could I forget the night you told me about our grandchildren?"

"You never said anything to tell me you'd remembered."

"I don't tell everything I know," she retorted loftily, then spoiled it with a giggle.

"Just like I've never told you that I know you did the designs for the Corbett Building that won your father the architect's award."

Caroline showed no surprise that he knew. "It was only my hand that did the drawing. The concept was his. I don't think what we did was dishonest."

"I don't think anyone would doubt your honesty. Now, back to the night of the four grandchildren, did you mean it when you asked me to come to bed that night?"

"Yes."

"A waste! All those weeks," Gabe groaned.

"We can make them up, after the christening."

"Why not now?" A wicked gleam was in his eyes as he rolled her neatly beneath him.

"We're going to be late."

"Doesn't matter."

"Gabe, Shiloh's coming," she protested halfheartedly.

"I know."

"And Scotty."

"Don't forget Hiram, and Riley, and Georgie Lee, and Butch, and Julie and Kevin and the twins, and Mable May and Harry."

"Mable May and Harry?" She would have sat stark upright but his arms held her too closely. "You invited Mable May? And Harry? Who are they?"

"Of course I invited them," he said smugly.

"Gabe!" She pummeled him on his chest. "Who are they?"

"Well. I really don't know, but they cornered me at the inn with pictures of their six children, so naturally

I had to tell them about our two. And that just naturally led to an invitation to the christening.''

"Naturally."

"Don't interrupt, love. Bragging fathers don't like it." He kissed her startled lips closed. "If I can listen to stories of their six children, they can meet our handsome cadet and the papoose."

"Do…" Caroline choked on the question. "Do you really talk to people about the boys?"

"Certainly. My best audience is Shiloh. In fact, I practiced on him by transatlantic call."

"You didn't!"

"I did." He grinned ruefully. "Not that I gave him much choice."

Caroline was suddenly serious. "I wish he had what we have."

"He will, love, someday. All it takes to settle a man down is the right woman. Look at me," he said piously.

"I'm the right woman?"

"For me you are. Now, where were we?"

"I think we were about to catch a falling star." Caroline lifted her mouth in an invitation Gabe had no intention of refusing.

A small breeze played among the trees. Tall grasses swayed before it and pines that hovered over the cabin whispered. From the sleeping loft of the cabin laughter rose, deep and light, and happy.

Gabe had promised her laughter with the kisses.

* * * * *

Take 4 Silhouette Special Edition novels
and a surprise gift
FREE

Then preview 6 brand-new books—delivered to your door as soon as they come off the presses! you decide to keep them, you pay just $2.49 each*—a 9% saving off the retail price, *with no additional charges for postage and handling!*

Romance is alive, well and flourishing in the moving love stories of Silhouette Special Edition novels. They'll awaken your desires, enliven your senses and leave you tingling all over with excitement.

Start with 4 Silhouette Special Edition novels and a surprise gift absolutely FREE. They're yours to keep without obligation. You can always return a shipment and cancel at any time.

Simply fill out and return the coupon today!

* Plus 69¢ postage and handling per shipment in Canada.

Silhouette Special Edition®

Silhouette Romance™

Legendary Lovers Trilogy

BY DEBBIE MACOMBER....

ONCE UPON A TIME, in a land not so far away, there lived a girl, Debbie Macomber, who grew up dreaming of castles, white knights and princes on fiery steeds. Her family was an ordinary one with a mother and father and one wicked brother, who sold copies of her diary to all the boys in her junior high class.

One day, when Debbie was only nineteen, a handsome electrician drove by in a shiny black convertible. Now Debbie knew a prince when she saw one, and before long they lived in a two-bedroom cottage surrounded by a white picket fence.

As often happens when a damsel fair meets her prince charming, children followed, and soon the two-bedroom cottage became a four-bedroom castle. The kingdom flourished and prospered, and between soccer games and car pools, ballet classes and clarinet lessons, Debbie thought about love and enchantment and the magic of romance.

One day Debbie said, "What this country needs is a good fairy tale." She remembered how well her diary had sold and she dreamed again of castles, white knights and princes on fiery steeds. And so the stories of Cinderella, Beauty and the Beast, and Snow White were reborn....

Look for Debbie Macomber's *Legendary Lovers* trilogy from Silhouette Romance: *Cindy and the Prince* (January, 1988); *Some Kind of Wonderful* (March, 1988); *Almost Paradise* (May, 1988). Don't miss them!

SRT-1

Silhouette Desire

COMING NEXT MONTH

#397 TO LOVE AGAIN—Lass Small
After a personal tragedy, Felicia's feelings were totally numb—and she intended to keep them that way. But Nate wasn't about to let a will of steel come between him and the woman he loved.

#398 WEATHERING THE STORM—Elaine Camp
Simon wanted no part of the past he'd shared with Marlee. But she had a foolproof plan to change his mind. Simon was no fool, and he found that together they could weather any storm.

#399 TO THE HIGHEST BIDDER—Cathryn Clare
Thrown together over possession of a New England farmhouse, Janni and Bart planned to battle it out. Though the house was collateral, they found they couldn't put a price on love.

#400 LIGHTNING STRIKES TWICE—Jane Gentry
Dr. Jake Rowan was back, but Attorney Nola O'Brien wasn't interested. He'd left her heartbroken, but now he was determined to right past wrongs—the answer was love!

#401 BUILT TO LAST—Laurel Evans
Pressures from her job had Allison Napoli looking for an alternative life-style, and architect Josh Fitzpatrick was just the answer. But could he convince her that home was where the heart is?

#402 INDISCREET—Tess Marlowe
When Terri Genetti was forced to close her business, she didn't know handsome entrepreneur Jim Holbrook was behind her problems. But Terri learned she could follow her heart without betraying her dreams.

AVAILABLE NOW:

#391 BETRAYED BY LOVE
Diana Palmer

#392 RUFFLED FEATHERS
Katherine Granger

#393 A LUCKY STREAK
Raye Morgan

#394 A TASTE OF FREEDOM
Candice Adams

#395 PLAYING WITH MATCHES
Ariel Berk

#396 TWICE IN A LIFETIME
BJ James